TWENTIETH-CENTURY GIRL

My Story.

TWENTIETH~ CENTURY GIRL

The Diary of

Flora Bonnington, London 1899-1900

By Carol Drinkwater

■SCHOLASTIC

To every young girl who has a special dream. Believe in yourself, work hard for your dream, and fight for it. Those dreams can change the world we live in.

While the events described and some of the characters in this book may be based on actual historical events and real people, Flora Bonnington is a fictional character, created by the author, and her diary is a work of fiction.

My special thanks to a great team at Scholastic, including Jill Sawyer, Lisa Edwards and Ali Evans. Thanks, as always, to my agent Sophie Hicks.

Scholastic Children's Books
Commonwealth House, 1–19 New Oxford Street,
London, WC1A 1NU, UK
A division of Scholastic Ltd
London ~ New York ~ Toronto ~ Sydney ~ Auckland
Mexico City ~ New Delhi ~ Hong Kong

Published in the UK by Scholastic Ltd, 2001

Text copyright © Carol Drinkwater, 2001

Cover image supplied by Popperfoto

ISBN 0 439 99941 3

All rights reserved
Typeset by TW Typesetting, Midsomer Norton, Somerset
Printed by Mackays of Chatham plc, Chatham, Kent

4 6 8 10 9 7 5 3

The right of Carol Drinkwater to be identified as the author of
this work has been asserted by her in accordance with the
Copyright, Designs and Patents Act, 1988.

Cadogan Square,
London, 1899

18th December 1899

I shrieked and then shrieked again; each cry growing louder and more fearful. I covered my eyes. I couldn't bear to look and then I uncovered them again because I couldn't bear *not* to look! Lord, I was *so* afraid. I truly believed that the oncoming train was heading directly at me and that it was about to run me down and kill me! It was thrilling, and so lifelike. I swear that if I had been blindfolded, then transported by carriage, escorted to my seat and only allowed to open my eyes when I was in my place and the lights had gone to pitch darkness, I would never have guessed where I was. Pictures in motion! Who would ever have thought that such a thing could be dreamed of or that the created images could make you feel as though what you are watching is actually happening and that your life truly is in danger?

Afterwards, in the carriage home, reflecting on what I had seen and that all the images had been dark grey, I said to Miss Baker – she is my governess and it was she who took me to the moving picture house – "Strange that there's no colour. The trees in the background of the pictures, as well as the sky above, they were all varying shades of grey. And there was no sound. You don't *hear* the whistle of the approaching train, you cannot *hear* the hiss of its steam, or the locomotive's wheels rolling fast along the iron tracks."

"That's right, Flora, you cannot hear those things but you *see* them, see them moving, just as if they were real."

It is curious and I don't quite understand it yet, but it's such an exciting world to be caught up in. Altogether we saw ten different sequences, each lasting about a minute. Oh, I want everyone to go there and experience what I have experienced: moving pictures!

19th December 1899

"The only sound is the live pianist who accompanies each moving picture. He varies his tunes to suit the mood of each piece. I think he is there to create atmosphere. You know, a bit of drama and then lighter music for the comical bits."

I was recounting my outing of yesterday to my

father, my sister, Henrietta, and also Grandmama during supper earlier this evening.

"Yes, I've heard about these flickering photographs," said Father. "I can't say that I really approve. I sincerely hope that Miss Baker has not taken you to some amusement arcade to view this exhibition. Where was it held?"

"Oh, Thomas Bonnington! Do, for heaven's sake, stop being so stuffy! Miss Baker is a responsible young woman and a fine governess."

"Mmm, she's too 'modern', in my opinion. I don't want her teaching my two daughters bad habits."

"The event was held in a hall off Baker Street. It was perfectly respectable, Papa," I replied, with lessening enthusiasm. Why is it that Papa always manages to make me feel that what I have done is wrong? I am sure he doesn't intend to be so cold or indifferent.

"I would never have agreed to go," Henrietta chimed in, and I wanted to kick her under the table. She is such a perfectly well-behaved young lady and she always sides with Father. The fact is they always seem to side with each other.

"Tell us everything about it, Flora, my dear. I am dying to hear!" cried Grandmama, who is fascinated by any new idea.

"Well, it consists of photographic images," I began. "They are projected one after another, very, very fast on to a blank screen. The speed makes them flicker and creates the illusion of movement."

"How can it possibly do such a thing?" sneered Henry. (Henry's my nickname for my horrid older sister!)

"What is the subject of these pictures?"

"Well, they are about all different things, Grandmama. But the one which made me jump out of my skin was of a locomotive train travelling right towards the camera. It was coming so fast I screamed, thinking that it would burst out of the screen and run me over!"

How my family laughed at me.

"Fancy being afraid of a photograph," scorned Henry, but I assured them that until you go and see it for yourself, sitting there in front of that giant screen, you cannot experience how *real* the motion of the pictures feels. According to Miss Baker, the idea was invented by two brothers in Paris who own the most successful factory in Europe for the manufacture of photographic plates and equipment. Their name is Lumière which is quite a curious coincidence because the translation from French of the word *lumière* is *light*, and you cannot make photographs without light!

(Miss Baker teaches me French and she was very impressed that I remembered the word from my book of nouns!)

It is going to be the entertainment of the new century, she says. Oh, I hope so. It will be much more fun than going to a magic lantern show or the circus. There is something about the circus which rather upsets me. It's hard to say why exactly because I love the smell of sawdust and I don't mind all that pushing to get to one's seat through the great press of ordinary working people, who are as excited as I am at the prospect of a show. And I love all the bands playing lively tunes, the acrobats turning somersaults; those are great fun. But it's the animals. Yes, that's it. I cannot bear to see all those poor elephants trudging around in endless circles, with a ringmaster holding a whip to their backsides, bullying the poor creatures into standing on their hind legs like hungry dogs begging for titbits.

Dear Miss Baker, it was so kind of her to take me along with her to the house of moving pictures. I shall have to find something very special to buy her as a Christmas present in return.

21st December 1899

Preparations are afoot for the festive season. I have strict instructions to keep Bassett, our hound, well clear of the kitchens where there is a bustle of activity. Three plump geese have been purchased by Cook. Tomorrow, Harrods will deliver them and they will be plucked and then stuffed with onions and chestnuts and other divinely delicious things for our Christmas lunch. And then, for the last night of this dying nineteenth century into which both I and my sister have been born, Papa is preparing a very splendid and divinely swish party. Henrietta will be eighteen in January so Papa has decided to end this year with a houseful of guests. It is quite unlike him. Usually, he buries himself in his work and dedicates his spare time to his boring old accounts. He rarely has time for us, his two daughters.

Later the same day

Whichever room I pass through, the sweet tangy perfume of tangerines fills the air. It is one of my favourite smells because it always reminds me that Christmas is here once more. We are promised "a white one" this year. Or so Jenny, one of our maids, informed me as she built up the coal fire in my bedroom hearth. She pronounces the forecast, in that strong cockney accent of hers which I could not even begin to imitate, with such delightful certainty that I would never dare question how she could be so sure of such a thing.

Miss Baker left this afternoon with her suitcase, off to the station to take the train home to her family in Shrewsbury. I wished her a splendid Christmas and gave her the small bottle of scent from Worth which I bought for her this morning.

22nd December 1899

"Rise and shine, Lady Flora Bonnington!" Jenny's plump cheeks were flushed with pride this morning when she came in to wake me. She pulled up the blinds, called me to the window and, when I peered out, I discovered that it was snowing! What a beautiful sight! And to complete the picture, a robin was perched on the outer sill, tilting his head and fluffing his feathers and strutting to and fro in a very self-important way, as though he had been there for ages, impatiently waiting for lazy old me to "rise and shine"! His were the sole prints in a deliciously crisp, white world.

"I told you, didn't I?" Jenny yelled, as she began to prepare my bath.

Our tree is being delivered before lunch and Papa has promised that it will be tremendously tall.

Grandmama, Henry and I are going to Harrods this afternoon to shop for presents and crackers and coloured-glass decorations to hang on our tree. After, Grandmama has promised us tall mugs of hot chocolate and cream puffs at the coffee shop across the street from the store. What a divine day!

I bought a journal and have begun to transfer all my scribblings of the last few days into it. It will record my journey into the new century. I shall call it "Twentieth-Century Girl", for that is what I intend to be!

23rd December 1899

There were secret comings and goings today as a large box arrived at the tradesmen's entrance and was instantly vanished away out of sight. I was in the kitchen at the time, starving and in search of a delicious snack, or I wouldn't have known a thing about it. Judging by the expressions on the faces of both Cook and Jones (he is our butler and a simply divine sport), and the general carry on, I am guessing it was a Christmas present for *ME*. What on earth could it be, I wonder? It looked heavy and was sort of squarish and large and, due to the manner in which it was being handled, I think rather fragile. When I asked Jonesy to give me a clue, he simply winked and trotted away.

I can't wait, I love surprises!

24th December 1899

Bassett is dozing on the rug in front of the fire. He is making funny snuffling noises and seems to be dreaming happily. It is late and I am completely exhausted, but I cannot sleep. Instead, I have been occupying myself with the joyfully secret business of wrapping my Christmas gifts: a leather journal for Henry (far more stylish than the one I bought for myself), a brooch for Grandmama, boxes of chocolates for Jenny and Anna and Cook, a hairbrush for Jones and a silver photograph frame for Papa. When all that was accomplished I curled up lazily in my nightgown on to this cushioned sill. Except to note these few lines in my journal, I have not moved from here these last two hours. I have no motivation to read and so have been staring out of my bedroom window on to the crisp tranquillity of Cadogan Square. Nose pressed against the cold steamy glass, I have been watching the comings and goings of strangers and neighbours and cherishing these hectic days and navy, starry nights because they are the very last I shall ever see of this century.

The clip-clop of the horses' hooves drawing late-night carriages filled with exhausted partygoers is muffled by the deeply lying snow. Passing pedestrians, tightly wrapped in extravagantly flowing fur over-coats, move swiftly towards their destinations while their breath rises like clouds of smoked tobacco towards the brightly burning, gas street-lamps. How I love London in winter! And how excited I am feeling.

Time is marching forward, carrying us over the threshold and pitching us, willy-nilly, into a new century. The prospect of growing up in that unexplored territory is so thrilling that I fancy, if I close my eyes tight, I can almost see the process taking place! The clock ticks, its hands turn, chimes ring out the hours, servants change linen, meals are prepared, footsteps creak on the landing, calls of "Goodnight" from the carpeted stairs: Christmas approaches like a cheery friend. A day slips away like sand in a sand glass and then another day dawns and so we are caught up in this inevitable passage towards 1900. And here I am, Flora Bonnington, being drawn helplessly along with it, whether I wish it or no. Oh, but yes, I do wish it, fervently. All my life save, for these first fourteen and a half years, will be lived out there, in the twentieth century. Exit 1899, enter 1900. How it makes me question my future. What will become of me in this soon-to-be-born century? Will I look back on these days as happy ones, remembering *me* before I grew up into a young aristocratic lady? Or will my life be snatched from me, tragically and without warning, like my darling mother who is and always will remain a stranger to me? Might I achieve great things and be applauded for my wisdom, energy and grace, like dearest Grandmama? Or will I follow in my father's footsteps and take the city by storm? I think I can safely predict that I shan't be going into business and making millions like Papa for I have no real head for figures and such matters are tedious to me. In any case, such opportunities are not available to women. We live in a world ruled and governed by men.

My father is Thomas Bonnington. He has his offices in the Square Mile of London which is the city's prosperous financial quarter. His company is named after him: Bonningtons. It is a well-known and highly esteemed import and export business, transporting

18

merchandise from the British colonies worldwide into London's Docklands.

As you might imagine, Papa is a very wealthy man. He is also a good and fair father and I love him deeply, but we do not think alike. It is not that we quarrel, it is simply that I feel I would have been better understood by my mother. In any case, he is so rarely available to us. He is too busy with his work as a merchant and a businessman. (Grandmama calls him a "gentleman capitalist"!) His ambitions for my future are not my own. He wants nothing more than to see me and my older sister, Henrietta, happily married, living in fine London homes, the toast of respectable society with upright husbands and families of our own. Henry dreams those dreams, too. But I am restless. I have longings within me. I want to do something special with my life though I have no idea what that *something* is. Just so long as it is exciting and I do not have to live a run-of-the-mill type of existence.

To be an artist or a bohemian or a campaigner, any of those would be marvellous, but the thought of simply being someone's wife fills me with a kind of horror. People tell me that I talk nonsense and that it is because I am too young to understand. When I meet the right man for me, they say, I will know it and be

19

happy. Even Miss Baker says such things, yet she's not married and she's already past 28.

Grandmama doesn't talk like the others. She listens to what I have to say and encourages me. I tell her that I would like to go to university and read languages or literature and she approves of that idea. In fact, she spurs me on. My mother went to university. She was part of the first wave of British women to go on to higher education. That was thanks to the vision and encouragement of my dear grandmother, Lady Violet Campbell, who lives with us in our five-storey home in Cadogan Square and about whom I shall write reams later. It is getting cold sitting on this windowsill, my toes are tingling and I am falling asleep. Tomorrow is Christmas! Hooray!

25th December 1899

Well, what a magnificent surprise!

The box I accidentally witnessed being delivered the other morning turns out to be our present from

Papa. It is to be shared by Henry and I, but will be for the pleasure of us all. What a moment when Father unwrapped it. He insisted on doing it, "in case we damaged it," he said. Then, he play-acted and staged the whole thing, just like a conjuror. At the very instant, the box-machine was revealed, Father called, "Hey, jingo!" and *orchestra music came out of it*. The gift wrapping fell to the floor, Bassett began tearing at the ribbons and papers and we stood in awe and amazement.

"I believe it's a phonograph, dears!" said Grandmama.

"Quite right, Violet, that is exactly what it is," said Father, smiling.

It really is a most remarkable invention. I had heard about them but had never actually heard one playing before. It is quite extraordinary to cluster around it in the drawing room and listen to sounds coming out of it. Music from a box! What a world I am growing up into! Here, in our very own home, we have a machine that plays tunes and only one week ago, I saw moving pictures without any sound. What a step it would be if, in this new century which awaits us, a method could be found to somehow gel these two discoveries together and create moving pictures with sound! But I fantasize! Perhaps I should grow up to be an inventor,

21

then I could create these ideas myself. Think how splendid that would be!

Grandmama has given me a most beautiful, leather-bound book of plays by a Russian playwright who I do not know but who is becoming highly regarded, she tells me. His name is Anton Chekhov. Henry gave me a very elegant tortoiseshell hair slide which should keep my wretched hair from always falling all over my face. Lovely presents, all of them. I feel deliciously spoilt. After lunch, Papa took Henry and I for a drive round Hyde Park in his new horseless carriage. Bassett came with us and barked and howled at everything and everyone, and made us laugh merrily. We saw several others with similar vehicles; they seem to be becoming quite the rage, and Papa hooted and we waved. It was rather like another boat passing by when you are punting on the river. Everybody honks and cheers and waves. It's quite curious really, but thoroughly enjoyable.

There were crowds of people about because, in spite of the snow these last few days, the sun was shining a gentle lukewarm. We were driving through a perfect, pure white world. There was snow on the grass and branches of the tall, spreading trees and the sky was streaky with milky-white clouds. Fortunately, we had wrapped up warm with dozens of scarves and fur mittens and rugs because this new vehicle is less protected than our old carriage. It catches the wind and is a blustery adventure, but also a thrilling one.

Hyde Park was wintry, but magical. There were many parties skating on the frozen water. Nannies sat nattering together on park benches, watching out for the skaters or wheeling small children in prams, young boys were throwing snowballs or building snowmen and I saw dozens of couples wrapped and muffled in woolly scarves to protect against the cold. How comical they looked, like tortoises standing on their hind legs, holding hands. Tranquil holiday pastimes. I felt exquisitely happy.

As I watched everyone and took in the passing sights, I was trying to imagine how it would be to make moving pictures of some of the scenes I was witnessing. A skater turning and falling on the ice, for example. But would that image be as dramatic and scary as the train driving into the camera? Or might it be a sight to make the audience roar with laughter? What does it depend on, I asked myself? The position of the camera? I long to learn more and wish I knew someone who could teach me.

Later, before tea, at Grandmama's insistence, Henry and I accompanied her on a brisk walk through the gas-lit streets to Brompton oratory to hear organ music by the French composer, Saint-Saëns. It was heavenly, but quite complex.

I am stuffed with good food, but not too much so. It has been a truly memorable Christmas Day.

26th December 1899

Curled up in the warmth of the drawing room, a fire crackling in front of me, I glance up from my book, out towards the tree-lined streets and crescents of London where snow is falling again and settling softly. I am reading my Chekhov. Marvellous scenes crammed with snowstorms and passionate emotions. Those Russian lives and their country *dachas* seem all the more real to me today because by looking on to that expanse of untouched whiteness beyond my windows, I can very easily picture all those Russian characters living out their hopes and despairs.

Grandmama tells me that, before too long, Russia will most likely fall into the hands of the working class.

She predicts that the farmworkers and servants will revolt and may grow violent – not unlike France towards the end of the last century, during the time of their Revolution. "Why?" I asked her.

"Because there is so much poverty and inequality between the landowners and the working people."

"Will they chop off the heads of the Tsar and his Tsarina," I asked her. "In the same way the French chopped off the royal heads?"

"It wouldn't surprise me, dear."

My grandmother was once a landowner of some standing but now she is a socialist, as my mother might have been had she lived. Grandmama hoots with laughter and accuses me of being preposterous sometimes because I describe her as a *revolutionary*. "You have such an air of the dramatic, Flora. I am a socialist, young lady, as I hope you will be when you begin to put your mind to such matters." She brought my mother up to believe in and fight for the rights of women but Mama died five days after I was born, so I never knew her. I was never given the opportunity to discuss with her what she thought about Grandmama's ideals. And I never discuss such matters with Papa because I suspect he doesn't approve. He always grows silent and serious when the conversation turns to such subjects, though to be fair to Papa, he never openly criticizes Grandmama or her ideas.

It was after the death of my mother that Grandmama sold her estates and came south to live with us, keeping only one large country house in Gloucestershire which is where we go for weekends from time to time.

28th December 1899

How I long for Miss Baker to return from her family holiday so that we can make another visit to the moving pictures. I cannot stop thinking of the experience and must learn more about it. Today, in Paris, four years ago, was the first public showing of the moving images.

Preparations for our end-of-year house party leave me no time to write more. I have a new dress. It is silk aquamarine. I am anxious about it because it feels horribly formal which is most unsuitable for me. I feel as though I must not move when I am wearing it, in case it tears but Jenny reassures me by saying, I look a "right royal treat"!

31st December 1899

Grandmother has gone to the Embankment, where the down-and-outs sleep, to dish out cups of steaming Bovril. I offered to accompany her but she would not hear of it.

"Why?" I protested. "Are you concerned that I would be upset by such squalor?"

"I do not feel a need to protect you from life, Flora, but your father requires your presence here. You must assist with the reception of guests. I shall be back well before midnight and not a soul apart from you and I will have noticed my absence."

Which, of course, is entirely untrue. Everyone will ask after her and Father will smile politely and tell the truth and our society friends will coo and judge Grandmama terrifically lively but eccentric, which she is. Still, few recognize her for her real worth except Papa who, though he does not agree with her politics at all, respects the mould my mother was cast from. In any case, no one could deny that Grandmama is intellectually brilliant and a force in her own right. She is a brave and independent woman. I often think that the loss of her only child must have caused her immense grief and much to reflect on. She never discusses these matters with me. I like to imagine that if my mother had not died she would have been like my grandmother. I can see from the photographs I have of her and the two portraits that Papa keeps in his bedroom that she was as elegant and handsome as my grandmother is.

I must stop writing and hurry downstairs for I hear Bassett barking, the chatter of arriving guests and Jones taking coats and greeting folk at the front door.

1st January 1900

Father invited a jolly group of people to our supper party last evening. Well, there were one or two old fuddy bores, like Sir Vincent Andersen, but not many. Amongst them all was a journalist whose name is Winston Churchill. I think Henry was rather smitten with him; she didn't take her eyes off him all evening.

I thought at first that if I were going to fall in love, which I'd really rather not, I might pick such a type. Not for his stature or looks but because he's a writer, well-travelled, and because he has an individual, thinking mind. Although, on reflection, Mr Churchill is rather fond of the sound of his own voice. Once he got going he talked unstintingly and did not seem to have a mind to stop. I think he has been a soldier but now he's a correspondent in South Africa, writing for the *Morning Post*. He referred on several occasions to his experiences in the Boer War. Father asked him his opinion of the young backbencher Lloyd George who vehemently opposes that war in Africa. Mr Churchill replied, "I believe it will not be long before he is a major player in mainstream politics. Yes, in my humble opinion, Mr Lloyd George will go far, sir." He went on to describe Lloyd George as a jolly good orator and said that you can't get far in politics these days without such an asset. The way he talked, I began to think he was practising for office himself!

Both he and Father discussed politics – for too long, in my opinion – and the mighty power and prosperity of the British Empire. My poor ears were ringing with it all. I was growing weary and drowsy, but then Grandmama returned and brightened up the evening.

She was looking flushed from the cold, but full of beans.

"I believe you are all acquainted with my mother-in-law, Lady Violet Campbell?" said Father, rising as Gran approached.

"Forgive my tardy arrival," she cried with gleaming eyes and open arms. She came straight to the table, gave both Henry and I a big hug, sat herself down and asked Jones to bring her a whisky. "Be a dear, Jonesy," she said to him, *sotto voce*, "and bring the old girl a large double."

Jones smiled and withdrew.

Her behaviour usually causes a flurry of interest – sometimes, shock – for some of her good works have been written about and certainly her politics are talked of.

"Do you not fear for your safety, Madam, alone on the Embankment late at night in the midst of so many cut-throats and ruffians? Surely, you will agree that it is no place for a woman and most certainly not an unaccompanied lady?" Sir Vincent Andersen, one of Father's business colleagues or competitors, whichever he is, quizzed her – rather too sharply, I thought. Gran sipped her drink and warmed her hands by the fire. Lord, she was excellent. Then, she leant across the table, elegantly caressing her fine pearl necklace with her long fingers, smiled disarmingly and enquired: "Pray, what, in your opinion, *is* the place for women in this mighty empire of ours?"

"Women, Madam?" he asked in a rather confused manner. I fear he is used to conferring only with gentlemen and Gran's forthright approach can be alarming.

"Do you not feel that as we sally forth into a new century, a new brand of woman is called for? Or would you feel safer if we all stayed home, checking our laundry lists?"

That stopped old whiskery Andersen in his tracks. His pink cheeks were flushed with temper. "Women belong at home, Madam. Every well-bred woman knows that her contribution is as a mother and a wife and that public office should be left to the gentlemen. My good wife certainly knows it," was his response. Meanwhile his plump wife blushed, nodded obediently and stuffed a hefty morsel of cherry pie into her mouth.

Grandmother smiled and said no more.

Then young Winston piped up. "What brand of new woman are you speaking of, Lady Campbell?"

"The pioneering woman who is fighting for our rights. One who is filled with the energy and enthusiasm necessary to create national awareness."

31

"I fear it is going to take a great deal more, Lady Campbell, than vociferous idealism, to make every girl and housewife reconsider her place in society."

"Well, I, for one, am not daunted by the work needed to achieve our goals. A new century is dawning, in 25 minutes it will have dawned, and I want every female, no, every citizen, to question and reject the world we are living in. Such pioneers of this new, twentieth century must needs be as brave as the soldiers you so loudly applaud, Mr Churchill. But we need something more."

"And what is that, pray, Lady Campbell?"

"We need to be angry and determined, at all costs, to shake up the fusty attitudes of this male-dominated society in which we women are kept down like lesser beings. Times are changing, Mr Churchill. Women are not objects put on this earth for the amusement and convenience of men. We never were. The difference is that now women everywhere are waking up to their potential and they are no longer willing to tolerate the situation."

Mr Churchill went pale with shock. As did several other guests. There was a certain amount of coughing and shuffling of chairs. I feared she had gone too far, but Grandmama was not to be deterred. Clearly, she was as impatient with the masculine chatter of wars and fighting and imperialism as I had been.

Smiling broadly, eyes twinkling, she sailed on. "Still, when my Twentieth-Century Woman has won the day, as she no doubt will during the early years of this approaching decade, I pray that she will enjoy the very same levels of freedom as you gentlemen cherish."

"I can envisage no such female," Sir Vincent cut in curtly.

"But of course, you can't, Sir Vincent, because you do not want to. Our Twentieth-Century Woman will be an inconvenience to you," said Gran with a smile. It was tremendous to listen to her argue her case without ever losing her cool or her grace or good manners.

Father rang for Jones and ordered the champagne. It was twenty minutes to midnight and I sensed that he was desperate for the diversion. Moments later, two of the maids came through carrying silver trays of crystal champagne flutes. These were distributed in silence.

"Thank you dears, Anna and Jenny. In this new century, what I wish for my two granddaughters here, as well as for those two young women who have just left the room, is that they will be able to hold their heads high, having won the right to vote for the government of the country in which they live,

Mr Churchill. And once they have the right to a voice in politics, then they can begin to take part in the governing of this country…"

"Grandmama, you talk as though every woman wanted the vote. Not all of us care for such a tedious responsibility!" It was Henrietta interrupting, in a very impatient manner. We have always been brought up to respect one another's opinions, never to cut them short, but Henry cannot abide it when Grandmama gets going on suffrage or social matters.

"Let your grandmother complete her thought, Henrietta," said Father without rancour.

"Thank you, Thomas. To me it is an unpalatable fact that Britain maintains the greatest empire this planet has ever known – we govern islands in every ocean of the world, have staked our Union Jack in distant outposts, somewhere in the region of 400 million people of every caste and colour are ruled by our Queen and her parliament, we build colonies and instruct on a world scale – and yet we do not regard women as equals."

"You exaggerate, Lady Campbell." This was Robert Booth talking. He writes for the *Daily Telegraph* newspaper. "In the last 40 years we have conceded the right to higher education for women and given several financial benefits. What more can women seriously desire?"

"The vote, Mr Booth. Women do not have the right to vote, and we cannot claim sexual equality. A delicate issue which I will not address in the company of young girls, but where is the enlightenment in such thinking, Mr Booth?"

"Pah! The vote is a dream, Lady Campbell. What do women know of politics and governments?"

Before this argument went any further, Mr Churchill tactfully intervened. "And you, Miss Henrietta, what are your thoughts on the subject, what do you wish for yourself in this new approaching century?"

"My interests and hopes are simple, Mr Churchill, and befit a young lady of breeding, though neither my grandmother or sister would agree with my sentiments. I dream of an honourable marriage and countless children but, before having children, I hope for a life of modish balls and weekends spent at the grandest of country houses with weekly visits to play golf at the links or promenades to the seaside."

"You have a daughter of sound mind, Thomas," declared Sir Vincent, rubbing his greying mutton chop whiskers. His wife nodded her agreement again but she did not speak for she was engaged in another slice of tart.

For my part, I felt ashamed for Henry. I caught the look in Mr Churchill's eyes and I felt sure that the picture she had painted would bore him to tears.

"And so I wish it for you," was his response. "For if your beauty is the mark of your power, then you will be free to command whatever your heart desires."

Henry grinned, melting at his words.

"And what of you, Miss Flora?"

"I should like to be involved in the making of moving pictures," I replied without hesitation. Mr Churchill looked most amazed. "Really, well that's a most unusual response. I believe they are all the rage in Paris though I have not seen any myself."

"Oh you must, sir, they will be the entertainment of the new century," which sent everyone around the table into gales of laughter. I have no idea why.

"You mustn't pay any attention to my young Flora, she is young yet and still a dreamer," said Father. Then the clock struck midnight and he asked Jones to put out the oil lamps and, when that was achieved, he rose to his feet in the candlelight, to propose a toast. What an impressive figure he was in his starched white evening shirt and bow-tie, his black coat and evening tails, standing in the dusky glow at the head of our dining table. Behind him, his shadow loomed tall and imposing and I suddenly felt sick in my stomach, believing that the day would come when I could not help but disappoint him.

"To my two daughters," he began. "May this twentieth century bring them both good fortune and the fine husbands and loving obedient children they both deserve. To all of us here, health and prosperity. And to our Queen, Victoria and her glorious British Empire."

Everyone rose. "The Queen," they roared.

I bowed my head. Into this new century I was about to pour my life. "Please, let me make good of it," I muttered to myself.

Outside, in Cadogan Square, a crowd of neighbours began to let off fireworks in the private gardens. They whizzed and whooshed past our windows lighting up each of the faces within the room with a rosy glow. All over London, fireworks were cracking, people were shouting and calling. I closed my eyes an instant, Flora Bonnington, I said to myself, may you grow up to be a fine Twentieth-Century Woman. When I opened my eyes, everybody in the room was moving between chairs, shaking hands and expressing goodwill.

"Come, Flora, let us offer our good wishes to the heart of the house," said Gran and she led me by the arm to the kitchen where Cook and Jonesy and Anna and Jenny were toasting one another with glasses of sherry. Cook's cheeks were as red as beetroots from all the roasting and basting and, no doubt, from the sherry. Gran stepped forward and gave each of them an embrace.

"Thank you for a very splendid evening," she said. "I wish peace and dignity and prosperity to each of you."

I think the tippling had loosened them up a little for they joked with her and told her what a fine but eccentric mistress she was and then we left them to their partying and returned to the guests.

Later, while Jenny unpinned Henrietta's hair, Henry sighed in a most lovesick manner and then asked me, "Do you think you could fall in love with that young writer, Flo?"

"Mr Churchill! He's far too old. He must be at least twenty-SIX. It is true that he is intellectually quite brilliant but he never stops talking. And besides what does he know of women apart from charming them senseless, which is probably the goal of every man?"

"Why must you always talk like Grandmama?" she cried and stormed from the dressing room in her corset and petticoats, leaving me alone with poor bemused Jenny who was helpless with a handful of pins and her work half accomplished.

2nd January 1900

I talked to a fascinating young man on New Year's Eve. I had no time to mention him in yesterday's entry. His name was Leonard something or other. He was very gangly and tall with sandy hair and a freckled complexion. I believe he said that he is reading Classics at Cambridge though I am not too sure because there were so many guests to talk to and remember. At first I did not pay him a great deal of attention, but then he returned to my remark about the moving pictures and claimed to have an interest in the subject himself. When I asked him if he had seen the Lumière brothers' exhibition, he told me that he had and has seen several others from their displays in Paris. It was Louis Lumière himself, Leonard informed me, who photographed the moving pictures I saw.

"The travelling train sequence is entitled: *Arrivée d'un train à la Ciotat*. Or in English, *Arrival of a train at Ciotat*. Louis Lumière is the driving force behind the whole enterprise. It was very realistic, don't you agree?"

"I do! I screamed loudly and felt quite afraid."

"Lumière used a special new camera which he has constructed at the Lumière factory."

I learnt from Leonard that they showed their moving pictures to a paying audience for the very first time at the Grand Café in the Boulevard des Capucines in Paris. It is proving to be an enormous success. Not only are there viewings in London now, but also in many other major European capitals. Even places as exotic and far afield as Mexico City and Alexandria in Egypt.

"Thomas Edison, I am sure you have heard of that man, Flora?"

"You mean, the American who invented the light bulb?"

"Yes, he did, as well as the splendid phonograph your father has been playing to us this evening. That's the fellow. He has been marketing a contrivance called the kinetoscope, more commonly known as the peep show. Well, he's very interested in this new type of camera. He wants to take it to America. In fact, this new apparatus is very similar to his kinetoscope but working at a higher stage of development," explained Leonard who spoke with as much passion and interest as I had been exhibiting. "Edison has built a small studio in the grounds where his laboratories are based in New Jersey, America. He calls the studio 'Black Maria'. There, he has been making moving pictures, each of which lasts about twenty seconds. Oh, I believe this moving picture business has far-reaching possibilities."

"So do I," I cried.

"It is already highly international. Exhibitions in Osaka, Japan and Melbourne in Australia, even Maracaibo in Venezuela. I can think of no finer way to work and see the world."

"I have been thinking the very same thing!"

Just at that moment Father approached us from amongst the chattering guests.

"Has our young Flora got you going on this moving picture craze of hers? She really is quite a fan of it. No lasting harm in it, I suppose, as long as it does not interfere with her education and she doesn't take it too seriously. It's important for young ladies to be able to amuse themselves, just so long as it is in a decent fashion."

And that put an end to our conversation because, once Papa left us, Leonard looked a bit awkward and moved on to talk to someone else, and soon after it was time for everyone to go home.

How I would love to own one of those cameras! I could never persuade Papa to buy me one for my birthday. They are surely exorbitantly expensive, and he does not consider it anything but an amusement. Anyway, perhaps there is only the one in the world and Louis Lumière must guard it jealously, which is precisely what I would do. But, oh, a moving pictures camera!

4th January 1900

I managed to catch Gran on her own this afternoon. She was in the drawing room and I invited myself to sit with her. I had been thinking about the debate at the table on New Year's Eve and I wanted her to tell me all about her experiences. "Gladly," she cried, squeezing my hand, and then rang for tea and scones.

Gran is a follower of the women's suffrage movement. Actually, she is one of the founding members of the London Society for Women's Suffrage which was created in 1867.

"I would like to be a Twentieth-Century Woman, Grandmama," I declared nervously. "I don't want to end up like Sir Vincent Andersen's wife. I want to achieve something special and wonderful with my life."

Grandmama placed her book on the arm of the sofa alongside her and looked at me intently. "I believe you will, Flora," she smiled softly. "You are a brave and courageous girl and that counts for a great deal. You remind me so much of…"

Tea arrived, brought in by Anna. Grandmama thanked her warmly and asked her if Cook would be kind enough to send us through some of her delicious biscuits.

I waited eagerly, bursting with curiosity. And when Anna had left us, I did not give Gran one second to pour our tea. "Of what, Gran?"

"Of Millicent. Your mother, dear."

"Was she brave?"

Gran nodded. "Brave and very beautiful. But let us talk of you. What would you like me to talk to you about?"

"First tell me, what does it mean exactly, the word *suffrage*?"

"Well, the actual definition of the word is to give support to, to vote for or side with. In our case, in this instance, women's suffrage is about females supporting one another. A suffragette is a female who is fighting for the right of women to vote. Some suffragettes go further – they want women to have the same rights as men; we call this equal rights."

"How did it get started in the first place?" I asked her.

"It is almost impossible to pinpoint these matters to one single date. I suppose, the movement began up north, in Sheffield, in 1851 when the Sheffield Women's Political Association was formed. While in the late 50s, here in London, I was involved with a very dynamic group of women who called themselves the Langham Place group. But suffrage really got going in the 60s."

"Why? Why did it happen then?"

"Women were – still are – dissatisfied with, and brought down by, the role forced upon them by a society which is ruled by men. As things stand now women are ruled by men. Men are the privileged class and women are cast as the lesser, the weaker of the two sexes, which is utter nonsense."

"Do you hate men, Grandmama?"

My question made her laugh loudly and she paused, stroked my head and buttered herself a scone. "Of course not, dear! There are many men I respect and admire. But there are, equally, many women who deserve to be respected and admired. Unfortunately, they are so rarely given the opportunities to achieve the goals they dream of in life, or of reaching their full potential, because the laws – laid down by men – do not allow them certain rights."

I chewed for a while thinking about what she was telling me. I dolloped a second helping of jam on my scone and tried to think it through.

"How did you get involved in the London Society?"

"Well, there we were, my dear Flora, in the year of 1867, awaiting an amendment to a parliamentary bill which was known as the Reform Act. If the amendment was accepted, it promised to give equal voting rights to women. But unfortunately the bill – voted upon exclusively by men, I hasten to add – was passed but without the change we so passionately had hoped for. A wider selection of men had been given voting rights but not a single woman. Lord, we were furious with Benjamin Disraeli, Chancellor at the time, and the government. It was so frustrating and upsetting because the matter was out of our control. So, we decided that it was time to go to work and create awareness amongst the female sex throughout the capital. Take power into our own hands."

"Was that the real beginning of suffrage?"

"It was not the very beginning but it was a turning point for us. Things began to change in the 60s. There were some marvellous women working with us; Florence Nightingale, Josephine Butler, Emily Davis to name but a few. I was living in London at the time. As I say, we were frustrated and felt betrayed by what had happened – or rather had *not* happened with the Reform Act, so a group of us founded the London Society. I suggested that we start writing pamphlets and hand them out wherever we could. You see, half the trouble is that so many women have never questioned their roles as subordinates of men. They are asleep, dear! Look at your sister, what a remark to make: Some women don't want the 'tedious responsibility'! If only she could understand that it is about so much more than simply being given the vote. Why, when I was a girl, and that is not as long ago as you might think, Flora, we were forced to stand up and fight for rights which you young things already take for granted."

"What sort of rights?"

"Property rights, higher education, admission to the medical profession, as well as sole custody of our own children."

"What does that mean, 'sole custody'?" I asked her.

"Up until fourteen years ago, the year after you were born, dear, if a man died and left children behind, his wife was not allowed to be the legal parent of her sons and daughters. Consider it a moment. A mother was obliged to continue her role as a parent alongside a nominated male who, in the eyes of the law, was the child's guardian."

"Why?"

"Women were not judged sufficiently wise to make the necessary decisions regarding the upbringing or education of their children."

Anna came through with the plate of biscuits. I was puzzling about why we are not thought wise. And when Anna had left, I said to Gran, "It seems a bit unfair and skewwhiff to me to refuse women the chance of further education and then tell them that they are not wise enough to look after their own children."

"My dear, you are a suffragette in the making!" she hooted. "How right you are. You see, it's a vicious circle."

I had finished my scone and jam so I helped myself

to one of Cook's ginger biscuits. She makes them herself and they are utterly delicious; chewy and not too hard or crumbly: just how I like them.

"And when you begin to look at the world from that point of view, Flora, you will see that the inequality does not rest only with women."

"What do you mean?"

"It applies to poverty and the poor, as well as to many of the colonial peoples who are ruled by our empire."

"I don't understand."

At that very moment Papa walked in. He was handing his cane and top hat to Jones and was looking harassed as he often does when he first arrives home from work.

"Good evening, Violet," he muttered solemnly.

I thought I should leave them alone, but I didn't really want to. I wanted to linger and talk, spend time with Papa. Still, in readiness, I placed my cup back on the table.

"Hello, Flora, are you leaving?" Papa kissed me on the top of my head but his mind was elsewhere and I felt as though he were telling me to go, so I rose obediently. Feeling a bit downhearted about being sent away, I glanced back at Gran and at Father who barely seemed to register my departure. "Can we finish our talk another time, please?" I asked her softly.

She smiled and nodded. "Most definitely, dear."

Alone in my room, I tried to figure out what Grandmama had meant about the colonial peoples, but I failed to find an answer so I lay on my bed staring at the photograph of my mother that I keep on my dresser. I felt proud and happy that Gran should judge me brave like my mother. If she were alive, I was thinking, I would want to make her so proud of me.

10th January 1900

My days are filled with lessons again. Christmas already seems so long ago. Grandmama runs around buzzing like a fly. Henry and Papa went to Gloucestershire for the weekend but I did not want to go. They took Bassett with them. Well, he is a hunting hound and it seems only fair to let the poor fellow run wild from time to time though I can't bear to think of him charging about with dead foxes or rabbits in his mouth. I was hoping Gran and I would have a wonderful time together chit-chatting and discussing all the things we fancied but she has been attending meetings and luncheons all over town. Twice this week, she has been at the Royal Geographical Society of which she is one of the very few women members. So, I have barely seen her. I hung about the house, and read. Felt a bit lonely.

20th January 1900

Miss Baker and I visited the Royal Academy this afternoon, and then we went for ices at Fortnum and Mason. That is the kind of schooling I enjoy the most!

25th January 1900

Henry's birthday. She is eighteen today. Gosh, eighteen; it seems so grown-up! She received a bouquet of red roses from an admirer and seemed thrilled by them. I teased her about having a beau which made her blush and giggle but she was irritatingly secretive about who the flowers had come from.

As a treat, Father took us both to a new play which opened just a few days ago at the Princess's Theatre. It is entitled, "The Absent-Minded Beggar" and is the story of an African Boer who falls in love with the wife of a British soldier. There was an awful lot of shooting and battle carry-on as the British soldiers defended the woman and fought the war. The audience stood and cheered at the end. It was a great success. I found there were rather too many gunshots for my taste and not enough ideas.

Everyone chatted loudly and merrily while they waited outside the theatre for their carriages. The Earl of Londonderry and his wife, who is very regal both in her bearing and her clothes which were all furs and satin, were amongst the audience. Father introduced us.

"Ah, yes Lady Henrietta Bonnington! You're coming out this year, I understand?"

Henrietta, who was a little daunted, I think, by such a very grand and haughty lady, only nodded. It is true though, she will be coming out this year, which means that she, like other young ladies of our class, will attend society balls and be presented to Queen Victoria.

"Then we must send you an invitation to our ball. Thomas, you have attended one or two of our little *soirées* in the past so you know the mix of people. Well, it will be a rather fine affair. At our address in Park Lane. Goodnight." And they swept off in one of the grandest carriages I have ever set eyes on. After, Father took Henry and I for supper at Claridges where several rather fusty-looking politicians were dining. I did not know who they were. To me they were just a table of ageing men in dark suits. Father went over and shook hands and shared a few exchanges with them, but he did not introduce us.

Later, as we undressed for bed, Henry declared that it had been a perfect day. As I was closing my door, Jenny hurried by carrying a vase. It was filled with the red roses. She was delivering them to Henry's room, no doubt destined for Henry's dresser. How silly of Henry not to tell me who they are from!

30th January 1900

I think I have discovered the identity of the flower-sender. His name is the Honourable Viscount Archibald Marsh. He is the dreariest of fellows, wet as a fish, and sports a *very unattractive* waxed moustache which sticks upwards like a pair of opened scissors. Henry met him at Grandmama's country estate in Gloucestershire a couple of weeks ago. Since her birthday, he seems to have popped up wherever we have been visiting. It's very irritating. He's like a retriever all set for the hunt. Actually, that's unkind because I really like retrievers!

"She's smitten, dear," whispered Gran after the three of us had returned from riding in the park where – guess what?! – we bumped into him again, or rather, he bumped into us. "Oh, haw, haw, I say, fancy seeing you here!" he chortled. It was SO PATHETIC.

Henry must be keen on him because she acts so silly in his presence – coy and girlish – and then giggles senselessly at every jest he makes. It's quite embarrassing because, truthfully, his jokes are neither witty nor ingenious. Then she becomes awfully cross and flies into one of her temper tantrums with me when I speak frankly about how ugly I find him and what a frightful experience it would be to be kissed by someone with such a stiff, pointed moustache.

"Won't it get stuck up your nostrils and give you a nosebleed?" I asked her, but she threw a book at me and told me to get out of her room. Love seems to be depriving her of her sense of humour. Gosh, I hope she isn't *really* falling for such a daft sort.

10th February 1900

Father had been expecting a rather valuable cargo – ivory, I believe – to arrive at the docks but due to rough seas the steamer was delayed. This morning he received a telegram to say that there has been another delay and the ship will not be berthing in London before the end of the month, at the very earliest. He looked very disturbed by the news. I wasn't quite sure why and did not like to intrude upon his thoughts to ask him.

11th February 1900

Yesterday, Henry snapped at me, twice, for calling her by her nickname.

"Why must you try to belittle me like that?" she cried.

"Like what?" said I.

"Calling me 'Henry' in front of Archie. Whatever must he think of me?"

I was taken by surprise because she has never objected before, but there she stood erect as a soldier, shoulders back, eyes staring like a barn owl, announcing in a very high and mighty fashion, "It does not become a young lady, Flora, to be thought of by such a boyish name. I am Lady Henrietta Bonnington and that is what you must call me, particularly in front of others." At first, I was hurt by her anger towards me but then I had to fight hard not to smile for I believe her change of attitude, these airs and graces, are the fault of this dreadful fellow, Archie Marsh. It's too silly for words. After all, she is only eighteen and will not even come out until the spring. I hope I shan't be so daft when I reach her age.

Grandmama says I shouldn't mind so. "It's natural, my dear Flora, to have one's head turned by a young man or two at Henrietta's time of life, though it's most important to bear in mind that we have not been put on this earth for the pleasure of men. We should not come alive like clockwork when any man looks upon us. There is far more to us than that." By "we" and "us" Grandmama is speaking, of course, of women.

13th February 1900

Henrietta's talk – I dare not think of her as Henry! – is all of dresses and the trip she will be making to Paris next week to be measured for her wardrobe. And balls. Her season of coming out balls is already being drawn up, for Father is quite determined that she be presented to the very best of society. He probably hopes that new company will take her mind off Archie Marsh. I certainly do.

She tells me that she intends to return from Paris accompanied by trunks laden with dresses which will make her "the very epitome of high society fashion". It seems to have entirely escaped her overexcited brain that every other young lady will also have been shipped off to Paris to shop!

Still, I have to admit that I am jealous not to have the opportunity to visit Paris with her. While she was being fitted and dressed by Worth, I would go in search of the moving picture houses. Oh, think how divine that would be.

15th February 1900

I hate this role of chaperone! If Henrietta is not allowed to go out with Archie on her own, why must it always be me who is dragged along for the sake of social decorum? I have spent a most disagreeable afternoon. Archie took us and his beastly younger sister, Lydia, to the famous Earl's Court Exhibition Grounds. It is perfectly enormous and covers some two dozen acres of land. Archie tried his hand in a shooting gallery called Boerland. There, with a gun, you could "take a snipe at the enemy", which is what he did.

I was heartily amused because most of his shots were way off the mark.

In another part of the grounds, in a huge theatre known as the Empress Theatre, we witnessed hundreds of savages from the African colonies presented in dramatic spectacles. Among them was a prince, a warrior chieftain, who – in real life – was taken prisoner in the war and brought over to England as a captive. The performance is intended to show to great effect Britain's triumphs in Africa. Amongst the other captives were quite a few women savages.

"I thoroughly enjoyed that," said Archie as we were leaving the show. "It seems to be a splendid way to show Londoners the importance of Britain's domination of those unschooled, dark-skinned savages. It certainly shows who's master and that's no bad thing."

"Oh, I so agree!" gushed Henrietta, almost before he had finished spouting his opinions.

"What ugly people they are, those savages," said Lydia. "I feel afraid to look upon them. They should be sent back to the jungle."

I could not bring myself to say anything for I found the very idea of exhibiting those people rather disgusting. After all, they are human beings. I felt sorry for those tribes men and women and I am not quite sure why it seems necessary for us to prove our strength by humiliating them. If I had my way, I would not allow such horrid, cruel exhibitions.

Yes, I know that I am bad-tempered but it is not for nothing. I cannot bear to see what is happening to my sister. She dotes on Archie. Well, that is her business, I suppose, but why must she deny her own personality in the doing of it? Whatever opinion he voices, she instantly agrees with him. It is as though she has absolutely no opinions of her own. Even when he talks nonsense, which, frankly, is frequently, she nods and swoons. He is so irritating and bossy!

Tonight, she came and sat on my bed and confided to me that she has fallen in love with him and she hopes that he will propose to her. I was open-mouthed. I cannot believe such a thing. The thought of becoming the sister-in-law of Archie Marsh! Oh, it would be a most awful business. I should be hauled off to social gatherings where I would prefer never to show my face and where I should be expected to smile, be friends with nasty Lydia and play the obedient young lady. I think I would rather run away. I should escape to Paris. I *wish* I could.

17th February 1900

"And when you begin to look at the world from that point of view, you will see that the inequality does not rest only with women. It applies to poverty and the poor, as well as to many of the colonial peoples who are ruled by our empire."

This is a quote of Grandmama's which I wrote in my journal in January. We have had no opportunity to discuss it since then, but I have thought about it and I wonder now about all that I saw at the theatre with Archie and Lydia and Henry. Could those shows be what she was talking about? I must ask her.

I feel bloated and tired as though I had been eating too much. My back is aching, too. It's curious. I hope that I am not ill.

18th February 1900

When I woke this morning, my thighs felt sticky and I found that I was bleeding. I was very alarmed until I recalled, ages ago, that Henry had experienced the same thing and she had been angry and weepy when I'd asked her about it. I wanted to speak to Gran about it. She was preparing to go out when I caught up with her.

"You look as though you have something very serious to tell me," she smiled as Jones helped her with her coat. "Thank you, Jonesy."

"I have no lessons today and was wondering whether I could spend some time with you."

"I thought you and Henry were going to Regent's Park Zoo with Archie and Lydia?"

I shrugged. "I'd really rather not."

"Yes, all those caged animals on show for a shilling a visit. I wouldn't want to either."

I stared at her. I hadn't been thinking about the animals, caged or not. I had been thinking about the thought of Archie and Lydia's company and how miserable and worried I was feeling. "Where are you off to?" I asked her, hoping she would invite me along. She took me by the hand and led me through from the hall into the drawing room. Once inside, she closed the door. "What is it?" she asked softly.

Tears welled in my eyes. They surprised me as much as Gran, I think. A lump stuck in my throat and I couldn't speak so I just shook my head. "Nothing," I murmured eventually.

"Must be something, dear," said Gran, pulling me to her and hugging me tight, which somehow made me want to weep all the more.

"I don't know. I can't explain. It's just... I..."

"Feel lost, confused, at sixes and sevens? Those sort of things?"

I nodded. "It's though I don't belong here." I wept.

"Of course, you do. But I understand your heavy heart."

And then eventually, I braved it. "I'm not very well," I whispered, feeling ashamed about what was happening to me. "There's something wrong. I fear it may run in the family because Henry has suffered from it, too."

"Good Lord, child, what is it?" Grandmama exclaimed.

When I finally managed to speak of what had happened, she stroked my head and said to me, "It's nothing to be afraid of. On the contrary, you can be proud. Now, you are a fully-fledged young woman." She called to Jones and requested that he cancel her carriage and ask Anna to bring us some hot chocolate and a plate of Cook's fudge. She took off her coat, flung it carelessly across one of Father's prized French armchairs and said, "It's time for us to have a nice long chat."

20th February 1900

Henrietta and Grandmama left for Paris this morning. I was in a blue funk all day. But my stomach pains have gone, which is a relief. The bleeding continues but I don't mind it now. It seems rather fantastical to me, the notion that I could give birth to a baby. I had been intending to mention it to Henry yesterday evening, I so wanted to tell her that I am a grown-up lady too, but she was flushed with talk of Archie and the zoo and Paris, so I will tell her another time. I am no longer such a LITTLE sister.

Miss Baker cheered me with exciting news. She has heard about a woman working over in Paris for one of the moving picture companies; her name is Alice Guy. She is the secretary of a man called Gaumont and is the *only* woman in the *world* directing moving pictures. How I wish I could be her! How frustrated I feel about not being able to visit Paris with the others, especially now that I am GROWN UP!

22nd February 1900

Weather vile: cold, damp and horribly foggy.

My day was cheered up by a really splendid woman who came looking for Grandmama and stayed to dinner. Her name is Mary Kingsley. She is the niece of the novelist, Charles Kingsley, and she is also a writer as well as a friend of Gran's. She is in London but bound for Simonstown in South Africa where she is intending to nurse Boer prisoners of war. What a brave and energetic person, I thought her. I could not help calculating as I watched her across the table, attired from head to foot in black, that my mother would probably have been about her age. Did they know one another? Might they have become friends? I feel sure my mother would have been as lively and high-minded; it is certainly how I picture her. Miss Kingsley published a book recently entitled *Travels in West Africa* which has made her rather famous and she has promised to send me a signed copy which I can keep as my very own. I told her that I would like to be involved with the directing of moving pictures.

"The directing of moving pictures?" she repeated in amazement.

"Yes." I assured her that the idea was not too fantastical. "I take my inspiration from and would rather like to follow in the footsteps of a woman called Alice Guy, who is working in Paris."

"Alice Guy. Her name is not familiar to me. I must find out about her."

"Perhaps, one day you would allow me to visit you in Africa, Miss Kingsley, and we could take moving pictures of everything you have seen and written about," I suggested to her. "I have learnt that the beginnings of this moving picture business was originally invented by a Frenchman, a scientist named Étienne Jules Marey. He intended the photographs to be used as a study for science. The idea was that by looking at the photographs displayed together in quick succession, the differing styles of movement in animals could be more easily understood. The word *cinematic* comes from the French and means the geometry of motion. It was his work, his research, that first inspired the Lumière Brothers."

"My word, you really have taken an interest in this!"

"Come now, Flora..." said Papa, but so carried away was I with my subject that I barely registered his warning.

"Oh, yes, Miss Kingsley, and I really believe that it would be possible to make moving pictures of animals and tribes in the jungle and, surely, these would be of interest to people who may never have the opportunity to go to Africa and see these sights for themselves."

"What a simply fascinating concept!" she cried. "To take moving pictures and document the lives and customs of the African tribes. Mr Bonnington, you have a very brilliant daughter!"

"Thank you," he said. "I fear that you may be right."

"Oh, do not fear it, sir. Intelligence and sensitivity in a woman are to be applauded and encouraged, not feared. And Flora seems to be richly gifted in both these qualities."

I was speechless and felt so proud I wanted to yell and shout. If only Gran had been there. Or my mother.

"Oh, dear," said Father, "I seem to be surrounded by what my mother-in-law, your friend Lady Campbell, describes as the 'Twentieth-Century Woman', and I am afraid that I do fear it. I fear that you will all be the undoing of me." He spoke politely – in fact, he was very charming to Miss Kingsley – but I worried that I had said too much. As she was leaving, Miss Kingsley expressed again how disappointed she was to have missed Grandmama but has promised to come and have dinner with us upon her return from Africa.

Father was not too distant this evening, but after Miss Kingsley had gone he told me that a young lady who talks too much is considered unattractive. "It is not polite, Flora, to hog all the attention when there are guests at the table. You really must learn your place if you are to do well in society."

I was wounded by his words but, on reflection, I am sure that he is right. I do get carried away with my ideas. Still, I feel hurt that he felt the need to chastise me so. I had thought that Miss Kingsley had been genuinely interested in what I was telling her.

23rd February 1900

All is not lost! Yesterday evening, Papa received a telegram to say that his long-awaited ship will be docking the day after tomorrow. During our dinner this evening, I begged him to take me with him to the port which he readily agreed to do. I think he knows how I love visiting the docks with all its bustle and busyness and mixture of faces and languages. I am only sad that I cannot take photographs and show them as moving pictures. I would like, as Miss Kingsley described it, to document the life of London's extraordinary port; our link with the rest of the world.

There are really only four companies, including Father's, who, between them, own the entire East End docklands. Father and two other companies have the north side of the Thames. Their lands stretch from Tower Hill, just beyond the city, right along as far as Tilbury. This area is known as the Docklands and is entirely situated on the banks of the River Thames. There is one other important dock site on the south bank of the river which is known as the Surrey Commercial Docks, but Father's company has no shares in it, nor does he own any land or warehouses over there. Everything Father owns is on the north bank.

I love to go and watch the cargo from Father's ships being unloaded on to the quays alongside where the ships have berthed. Papa owns literally miles of three- and four-storeyed warehouses behind the docks of Limehouse, Albert and St Katherine's. These are where he stores his valuable cargoes. If you have never been inside a warehouse you would be amazed. They are huge cavernous storage spaces set back from the river. It is like visiting Aladdin's cave because you walk in and you are instantly hit by the various scents of dozens and dozens of unfamiliar, exotic produce. There is nowhere else I have ever been in London that has such a curious mixture of smells and perfumes. Once you begin to look round you find yourself surrounded by treasures of every imaginable kind; chests of fine-leaved Indian tea, for example, or gold coins from Australia or gold bars brought over from the mines worked by the natives in South Africa, sugar from the plantations belonging to British island colonies in the Caribbean, bales of cotton, crates of Jamaican rum, spices, peppers, wood and many, many other delights; all waiting to be sold or collected. Standing in one of the warehouses with your eyes closed and breathing in those scents or opening your eyes and staring at the weird-looking fruits with names like pineapple, even though they don't even vaguely resemble pines or apples, is like being transported to somewhere you will probably never visit in your whole life.

Back out on the quays, once Father's ship has been unloaded and has been left empty it is ready to be cleaned and prepared for its next departure. Then the vessel will be restocked by the stevedores. Stevedores are dockers specially skilled in the business of ship-loading. Many of Father's ships carry silver bars and silver coins bound for the colonies of Hong Kong and Bombay, India. These are heavy and valuable cargoes. A vessel which is unevenly loaded runs the serious risk of capsizing out at sea in stormy weather, so being a stevedore is a job of enormous responsibility. Father transports an assortment of British goods out of

England, as well as in to it. They are destined for dozens of exotic ports as far-flung as India or China. Father's main business is importation but he exports produce for two reasons. The first is that if the ships travel across the seas empty – en route to collect cargo – it costs money, so it is better to load them and make money in both directions. Secondly, the import business in London is not quite as healthy as it was fifteen or so years ago. Father says that all the major traders are aware that their profits are not as handsome as they were ten years ago.

Although there is competition between Bonningtons and the three other major import companies, Father's main adversaries have become the small wharf businesses. Also, the ports in the cities of Liverpool and Bristol are expanding rapidly. Both of these dock sites have been modernized which means they are now able to accept the latest steamers and ocean-going vessels. Even those ships which are so substantial and cumbersome that, until recently, there was no British port other than London that was wide enough and mechanically sound enough to berth them, can now be berthed in Liverpool or Bristol. These modern advances taking place outside of the capital are unfortunate for Father because it means that London is losing some of its share of the import trade.

Still, I don't think he is really concerned about it. He has a whole fleet of ships of his own, acres and acres of four-storey yellow brick warehouses and the land on which they stand so, whatever happens, he will always have a thriving business.

25th February 1900

Papa and I set off directly we had finished breakfast, which was my favourite: kippers and scrambled eggs and lashings of hot buttered toast laden with home-made marmalade. Cook said we needed a good hearty meal, to keep the chill off us. "It comes in on those winds down by the waterside. You'll catch your death, if you don't eat right." I begged Father to allow me to take Bassett with us but he wouldn't agree to it because, he said, the dog would cause chaos on the docksides, which is probably true. So, the dear hound stayed in my room, looking very glum. He probably felt as miserable about seeing us go out as I did, watching the others depart for Paris, full of *joie de vivre*, without me.

Papa and I motored together, laughing like carefree chums, in his automobile. I felt so happy that his upset towards me of the other evening seems to have been forgiven. It was a fine morning, not too blustery. We took the route along the Strand passing the Gaiety Theatre. As we neared the Aldwych, Father slowed and pointed out to me where the proposed new north-south avenue is to be constructed. It is intended to link Waterloo with King's Cross, if our Lord Mayor and the London County Council ever agree on the architect and designs, that is. Father said that there is a great deal of indecision on the matter.

We passed along through to the city where Father's offices are, passing by Mansion House, the lord mayor's residence, towards Tower Hill and made for the docks from there.

When we arrived at the port, there were dozens and dozens of labourers, many of them bare-torsoed dark-skinned men, unloading chests from the holds of five other steamers belonging to one or other of the rival import companies. There was coffee and sugar, from Java, I believe, and massive trunks of ivory – African elephants I would guess judging by the size of the pieces – wooden chests of Indian tea bearing the lettering *Darjeeling*, a heavily guarded shipment of gold from South Africa and another of spices from Ceylon and the South Sea islands of Fiji.

One shipment, which must have come in from Africa, was disembarking live, wild animals. Such cries the creatures were letting out. Roarings and screechings (just as well I didn't bring Bassett!). I found it distressing to see monumental jungle beasts such as elephants being pulleyed helplessly off the decks while folk stood around oohing and aahing and gawping. It was worse than the circus. There were cages with lions in them, too. And though, on the one hand, it was extremely exciting to see creatures in the flesh that I recognized only from drawings in books, it was a horrid sight to see them with their power and majesty all trussed up. It brought to mind a line of Rudyard Kipling's which quite touched me when I first read it, "that packet of assorted miseries which we call a ship". Perhaps Kipling's words affected me because my own father owns so many seafaring crafts though, thank the Lord, I have never heard Papa speak of transporting live creatures.

"See there, Flora, there's our vessel." Father had moved away from my side and was calling to me and waving from further along the quay. I ran to where he was standing and there at a distance riding the muddy

Thames water was the looming silhouette of the steamer, SS *Victoria*.

It is such an impressive affair when a huge ship approaches the docks. It always makes me feel so small – Alice in Wonderland-like – and unschooled in the secrets of the world. My heart never fails to flutter at the thought of all the seas the watercraft has crossed and all the different peoples it has carried. I so long to be one of those passengers or sailors standing on the upper decks, leaning against iron railings, watching the sight of land grow closer. Dreaming thus, suddenly I thought of the moving pictures again. What would it be like to have a camera up there with me, to document our arrival!

At the ship's side, small tugboats were spinning and turning like harassed insects engineering those final moments of safe passage. Then the dock gates opened, as if by magic, and the ship glided majestically and surely to its berth. What an achievement! After all those months at sea, all those storms and rocky passages, all those dangerous capes, all the scary moments of wondering whether the cargo will ever safely reach its destination and then the anchor is lowered, sinking to rest in the thick slimes of mud on the bed of the Thames, and the vessel rocks imperceptibly to a standstill, mission completed! Hoorah! Bravo! I longed to cry out, but no one else seemed to think the moment particularly special so I kept silent.

Perhaps, I should decide to earn my livelihood as a ship's captain but, alas, that is not a profession for a woman. *And why ever not, I ask myself?*

The sailors, of course, were disembarking as swiftly as they could. They are always desperate to stretch their land legs after so many months at sea and in many cases to hurry home to wives and families, but the craft was not deserted for more than a few minutes because almost as soon as it was moored, swarms of impatient stevedores began to climb aboard, beginning the process of unloading the precious cargo.

Within no time, the quay was laden with produce which was being sorted and listed before being trucked along the jetties to our warehouses where the merchandise is catalogued and then stored.

I have never before stopped to consider the labour force involved in such an enormous enterprise as Father's. Where do all these men come from? I noticed that not a few of them were negroes as well as several other types of colonial peoples, many of whom are not Christians for I have heard tell that they practise strange religious rituals on the docksides. I would have dearly liked to have engaged a few of them in conversation and learnt from them how they came to be in England in the first place and from which corners of our empire they have originally hailed. But it would not be considered ladylike or dignified for a young woman of my background to speak to such men, and my behaviour would certainly anger my father.

Still, I sincerely hope that their working conditions are not as the Kipling quotation describes, "a packet of assorted miseries".

While I was musing on all these matters and as we were making our way from the dockside back to where Father had parked his automobile, my attention was drawn by a cry of distress coming from somewhere distant from where we were.

"What was that?" I called to Papa who continued to move towards the gates. I paused and looked back and caught sight of a policeman engaged in what looked like a scuffle with a scruffy, bearded man who I took to be a docker. Two more policemen were running to join the first and back him up. I ran and grabbed Father by the sleeve. "What's happening?" I asked him. He barely glanced back.

"Life on the docks, Flora. Nothing to concern yourself about." But as he said these words the three bobbies grabbed and held fast the man who had been shouting.

By this point he had been rendered helpless as they pressed him hard and beat him on his back. His knees began to buckle and he fell forwards, hitting the cobbles with a thud and a groan. Driven to the ground, balanced on all fours like an animal, the policemen continued to hit him and kick him in the ribs.

"They're hurting that man!" I cried, without thinking. "We have to do something. Papa!" My father continued on towards the exit to the dockside.

I stood my ground. "Please wait, Papa," I cried again at which my father stopped and retraced his steps until he reached my side.

"What is it, Flora?"

I was fighting to catch my breath.

I think Father was most amazed and shocked to see how upset I was about the incident taking place. The man was now being forcibly dragged by the bobbies away from the dockside. He was not going peaceably and I noticed another blow or two fall upon the back of his head. He yowled with pain.

"Stop!" I yelled, but they were now beyond hearing me.

"Come, Flora, don't upset yourself. The man is a low thief and probably a drunk into the bargain. We must go." Papa took me gently by the arm and led me away.

"You really mustn't be so sensitive. It will be the undoing of you. Men who have done wrong must be punished."

"But what could he have done that is so bad to warrant such a beating?" I entreated, but Father was no longer listening.

When I glanced backwards, there was no further sighting of the quartet of men. Still, I was left feeling troubled and upset by the cruelty I had witnessed. All the way home, I remained silent, which suited Father who was miles away in his own thoughts. I stared out of the automobile at the passing streets fighting back tears, feeling so miserable at the prospect of returning to a house which did not contain Grandmama to whom I would have rushed in search of an explanation or, at the least, a huge hug and companionship.

26th February 1900

Grandmama and Henry are back from Paris, full of beans and stories. I was so OVERJOYED to see them. This evening at dinner, Henry talked of nothing but the grand stores and the designer houses and the splendours of the Seine river lit by gaslight. She said the train station, the Gare du Nord, was the most magnificent she had ever set eyes on. I refrained from pointing out to her that she hasn't seen all that many but she would have accused me of being jealous, which I was and, in any case, I did not want upsets. I wanted us all to be happy and to be like a real family.

Grandmama brought me delightful presents including lavender toilet water and a choker-necklace and then, with eyes beaming, she gave me the prize. The present that she knew I would treasure above all others. Leaflets about the moving pictures. She had taken the time to visit the Society for the Encouragement of National Industry to find out more information for me. I hugged her so tight for the trouble she had taken and for thinking of me when she could have been having a wonderful time.

"We did have a wonderful time, dear, but it doesn't mean we have to forget you."

Henry told us that they had lunched at a brasserie which, she explained, is a very informal eating house on the south side of the river, known as the left bank in a district called Montparnasse. "It was filled with starving artists wearing funny flat hats and clothes stained with paint. All bohemians, and I thought it simply horrid, but Grandmama loved it and she felt sure that you would too, Flora. Father, you wouldn't have liked it one little bit."

"No, you are right, Henrietta, and I rather disapprove of your grandmother taking you to such an establishment. But nothing I say will discourage you, eh, Violet?"

"It's important to know how other folk live. In any case, it is a perfectly respectable establishment, Thomas, dear."

"Oh, when can I go, Papa?"

I caught a conspiratorial look exchanged between my father and my grandmother and I knew instantly that they must have discussed the matter.

"Can I go?" I cried.

"We have to return in a fortnight to collect the dresses that are being made for Henrietta. Of course, we won't need to stay so long. A day or two at the most..."

"Unless, of course, they don't fit me."

"And why wouldn't they?" laughed Grandmama. "They are being made by the finest couture houses in the world."

"Yes, but I was measured before we ate so many French meals," wailed Henry. "I must not eat another thing before the Court Ball is over! Queen Victoria is going to take one look at me and judge me the plumpest of partridges."

"Don't be ridiculous, dear."

I waited, bursting with impatience for this exchange to end, forcing myself not to butt in or push my luck until eventually, I could wait no longer. "And may I accompany you, then? May I, Father? Oh, please, I beg you, let me go with them!"

"I don't see why not. Actually, I think it might do you the world of good. It seems to me that you spend too much time alone and thinking," he smiled. "But no artists' cafés on the left bank, do you understand, Violet?"

I threw my napkin into the air which produced tuts all round, but I didn't care, and I rushed from my seat and hugged my father so tightly, in a way I rarely ever do. "Thank you, thank you so much."

Alone, in my room, Bassett snoring soundly on the bed at my feet, I simply cannot sleep. I am bursting to tell Miss Baker my news. "I AM GOING TO PARIS AND I WILL VISIT ALL THE MOVING PICTURE SHOWS!!!"

27th February 1900

Reading, I discover that the camera used to photograph the moving pictures was patented by Louis Lumière in 1895 and he has named it the cinematograph.

28th February 1900

This is fascinating! Two years ago, according to an extract from an American science journal, a Monsieur Camille Flammarion undertook to cinematograph the sky. On a clear night, he takes up to 3,000 photographs. Does that mean that you can see the sunset happening all at once? The stars coming out? See the moon rising and waning? My mind is shooting like fireworks with the possibilities of cinematographing moving objects. Then, why not people, too? Think how it would be if I had my very own camera. I could cinematograph our trip to Paris and then show it to Father. Of course, it would not be quite so simple because I would need to have another apparatus, a form of magic lantern, to show the pictures and a dark room so that the flickering images could be seen to best effect. But, IF I had all those things, I could reproduce the trip and show it to Father, or to anyone else. The point I think I am trying to get at is that these cameras could show images of objects, scenes and events to people who would not otherwise be able to see them. Rather like writing in this journal and then sending it to someone to read but, instead of words, I would use moving pictures.

I could become a journalist, like Miss Kingsley, but with photographs. But who would want such a person? Certainly not the newspapers who use drawings rather than photographs.

1st March 1900

In all the excitement of my presents from Paris, I had forgotten to mention to Grandmama that Mary

Kingsley had dined here with us. Gran was most upset to have missed her and described her as "a rare and extraordinary woman".

"Her uncle, Charles Kingsley the novelist, was one of the original supporters of our suffrage movement, did she tell you that?"

I shook my head.

"He was among those who were instrumental in the bringing about of the Married Women's Property Act of 1870. This was the first of three acts which eventually gave women the right to their own property and possessions instead of everything being held in the name of the husband."

"How did you first meet her?"

"Goodness, our paths have crossed all over the place. I don't remember, but when the Royal Geographical Society agreed, finally, to open its doors to women and allow them to become members – a decision, I hasten to add, which was debated and fought over by all those silly men who then changed their minds and withdrew the right to female membership. Anyway, before the decision was revoked, I was invited to be among that first handful of women who were given membership. Not so long ago, Mary came along and gave us a fascinating talk about her travels in Africa and about the effects of British rule on that continent. Although to be quite fair, she has never approved of women accepting membership to long established men's clubs, even those with a particular purpose such as the Royal Geographical Society. Still, she and I immediately saw eye to eye. She, like me, I am happy to say, is not a hundred per cent in favour of all this tedious flag waving by 'the world's greatest empire'. Certainly, we British have done good but it seems to me and to Mary, who has travelled a great deal more than I have, that a certain amount of damage is being done as well…"

"What sort of damage?" I interrupted, feeling quite shocked by Gran's remark, for everyone I know agrees that Britain is the saving force of the world. Papa certainly believes it and *The Times* newspaper always boasts about it.

"You know that there is much about our British society that I do not approve of, Flora. The lack of women's rights first and foremost. It is as I have tried to explain to you once before. Any form of domination, whether it be male over female or rich over poor is, in my opinion, against the basic rights of human beings, Flora. So, the fight for the vote, for women's equality with men has become a political issue."

I thought about the man at the dockside. That image

of him being kicked like a dog came back to me but I decided not to mention it. I felt that to tell Grandmama was, in a way that I cannot quite explain even to myself, a betrayal of Father.

14th March 1900

PARIS. Finally, at last! We have arrived after a tempestuous boat journey and then a train ride from the port of Calais which was quite rocky but great fun. We are staying at the Hôtel Ritz. Lord, I have never seen such sumptuous luxury! I feel most out of place and want to whisper all the time. Everyone we pass in the lobby must be a king or potentate, I am sure of it. It is rather like being in a fairy story and I am quite swept away by it all, being not quite certain whether it makes me uncomfortable or not, but Grandmama promises that there are many places to visit in this city and they will be of a very different complexion. From the little I have seen out on the streets, it is a very pretty place. It seems to be smaller than London, more compact. There is a river, called the Seine, which runs right through the centre of it and divides the city into two; the left bank of the river which is south and the right bank which is north. I wonder if they have mighty docksides here, like Papa's. I wonder if he misses us; all his "young ladies" gone. He is probably too busy to notice.

Gran took us to dinner at Maxims restaurant which opened last year and has become very fashionable. Everyone was very chic.

15th March 1900

Yesterday evening, at dusk, when all the shops were closed and there was simply nothing left for Henrietta to buy, we took a fiacre – these are four-wheeled box-shaped coaches which are for hire everywhere. They are named after the Hôtel Saint-Fiacre in Paris where they were first used. Anyway, we took a fiacre to the Musée Grévin. There, they are giving shows using this new style of film exhibition. It was rather basic and, I felt, disappointing. It did not excite and open my mind in the way that I dream is possible with these moving pictures, but it was worth a visit none the less.

We learnt that these cameras, the cinematographs, are not available for sale, which was why what we saw at the Musée was not of the same quality. The Lumières guard the cinematographs for their exclusive use. The moving pictures they have photographed are not for sale either. They are rented out all over the world along with an operator who works the apparatus which shows them. This machine is called a projector and the man who operates it, a projectionist.

Other people who are interested in pursuing the moving pictures are building their own cameras or commissioning someone to build them on their behalf because they are impossible to buy. For example, there is a very famous French illusionist whose name is Georges Méliès. He owns the Robert-Houdin Theatre in Paris and, in order that he can record performances of his shows, he has ordered one of these cameras to be built for his exclusive use. He has also constructed a big glass house in his garden which he calls a studio. In this glass house he creates his moving pictures. Last year, he photographed a moving picture which lasted for THIRTEEN minutes and was a newsreel of a real event. It was titled, *The Dreyfus Affair*. Also, Monsieur Méliès *works with women*. I must remember this and IMPROVE MY FRENCH!

16th March 1900

Where to begin to recount the joys and adventures we have enjoyed during these two crammed but too short days in Paris? Now we are in the train on our return journey to the coast of France and, very soon, it will all be over, but it will NEVER be forgotten. There was shopping, of course, which did not greatly excite me but I am pleased with the new winter coat Grandmama bought for me. Henrietta, quite rightly, is laden with outfits and necklaces and gloves and perfumes and feathers and hats; all for her coming out which is to begin in a few weeks.

Watching her now across the carriage, she has flushed excited cheeks and a very glamorous new curly style of hair. She has barely mentioned the name of Archie Marsh, so I feel sure that Papa's decision to give her a very splendid coming out is the perfect plan and will introduce her to many other far more interesting people. And then I won't need to be the sister-in-law of such a buffoon! Lord, she would hit me if she read these words, but I mean her no ill. She is my big sister and I love her. It's her foolishness that makes me impatient. But enough of all this, I want to write about Paris and our splendidly exciting expeditions.

Yesterday morning, after breakfast, one of the concierges working in the reception of the Hôtel Ritz told Gran about a man named Pathé who has made a great deal of money out of selling phonographs, but also has an interest in the moving pictures. Because he was unable to buy any cinematographs from Lumière, he commissioned a man named Joly to build him a model of his own. So, while Henry was busy with the dressmaker who was putting the final touches to her ball gowns, Gran and I went all the way to Vincennes where we were told this Monsieur Pathé has his business but we were unable to find him. I was very disappointed. So, then we took a fiacre to another location where there are studios owned by a man named Monsieur Léon Gaumont. Gaumont's studio is where the woman director, Alice Guy, directs pictures but, alas, we were not able to meet with her nor see any of the material she has photographed. For some reason, it was a day off. Still, it was very exciting to be shown around. The studios were surprisingly basic. They have an open-air stage area about the size of our drawing room and another, covered area where they store items known as "props". The word "props" is an abbreviation of the word "properties". Properties are the articles used in the pictures. Chairs, for example, or swords and feathers and a few old battered helmets. It was a curious collection of items. The very notion of props struck me as curious. I had simply never considered that someone making moving pictures needs to collect things to create the world of the moving picture but, now that I have learnt that fact, it seems rather obvious.

I suppose I had simply assumed that every moving picture was a true reproduction of what was actually happening in front of the camera. It had not occurred to me that the director or camera operator is capable of *creating* the world that they cinematograph. This must mean that stories can be invented and filmed. So, it must be rather like storytelling in books except that photographs are used instead of words. It is not necessarily a form of journalism.

The most breathlessly exciting moment came when

we were shown the famous cinematograph camera. It was all wrapped up in black velvet cloth as though it would be damaged by the daylight. I was very taken aback when the gentleman showing us around unveiled it because it appeared to be a frightfully complicated contraption. I asked the monsieur – with the help of Gran's French – to explain it to us but he shrugged and said that he did not understand it at all. He was only the caretaker of the studio.

If Father ever did agree to buy me one, I am not sure that I would know what on earth to do with it. Still, I do long to find a place for myself in this world of cinematographs. The more I learn, the more exciting the scope of it becomes. I just cannot see how it could ever happen. I fear it will always remain a dream.

Later in the day, while Henrietta was *still* occupied with her dress fittings and matching her accessories – Lord, I shall never agree to all this coming out – Grandmama and I took a stroll to the quays where wonderful men in berets were sitting on stools making sketches of the water and the bridges and the tall, leaning buildings. As well as the artists, there were dozens of bookstalls. All of them were situated along the length of the riverside with the cathedral of Notre-Dame as a backdrop. It was a beautiful sight. There, they were selling parchment-yellow posters of Parisian theatre shows and antique books, several with very ornate gilt covers. It was too magnificent for words. I wished that my French had been good enough to investigate the books but I was a stranger to all their secrets. Miss Baker will be delighted to know that I have finally understood the point of reciting all those infernal French and German verbs. Languages are the tools for communication! Grandmama, of course, nattered away with all the stallholders just as though she were a French native. While she talked, I browsed and, suddenly, at one of the farther stalls, I caught sight of a poster. It was pegged to a line, which reached across the stall like washing hanging out to dry. Written across the poster in large letters were the words: CINÉMATOGRAPHE LUMIÈRE. Even with my hopelessly basic understanding of the French language I could not fail to comprehend the meaning of those two words! I moved up close to study what it was about and, lo and behold, what a wonderful discovery I had made. There, on the poster, was a sketched reproduction of six people seated in a theatre in front of an open curtained screen. They are animated and falling about laughing, staring at an image which is being projected on to the screen. Alongside these audience figures stands a boy in a uniform, rather similar to that of a bellboy. He is laughing, too. The moving picture they are so amused by is entitled *L'Arroseur Arrosé*, which, when I shouted to Grandmama to come and look, she translated for me. Literally, it means, "The Waterer Watered."

"I saw this picture," I cried, "with Miss Baker in London!"

The image on the screen is of a gardener holding a hosepipe which is spraying water all over his face and, in the background, a mischievous-looking boy is running away, triumphant.

The stallholder explained to Grandmama that this little story was one of the original examples screened at that first public exhibition in the basement room of the Grand Café in the Boulevard des Capucines in 1895.

"The audience are laughing," I jumped in to explain, "because the boy has deliberately trodden on the hosepipe and blocked its flow of water. When the gardener lifts up the nozzle to examine what is wrong with it, the boy steps off the pipe and runs away, leaving the poor man soaked in water. It is very funny."

"This poster is a memento which will be worth keeping," added the salesman.

"Really?" I cried. "Have you seen the film, too?"

"Me, *hélas*, no, but on that very first evening at the Grand Café when each member of the audience paid a franc, a programme of ten different films, lasting a total running time of 25 minutes, was shown. This moving picture was among that ten. How the audience laughed! And what a success! Within no time, the brothers were giving twenty screenings a day with long queues winding along the streets of Paris. Now they show their moving pictures everywhere in Europe. Ah, they are magnificent these brothers, Lumières."

"Actually, forgive me for disagreeing, but there are screenings all over the world now. Pictures in motion have become a very international affair." I was almost hopping with excitement and begging Grandmama to translate for me. Grandmama laughed and told the rheumy-eyed man what I had said. He nodded, looking impressed that I should know so much.

"Would you like this as a souvenir of our time in Paris, Flora?" Grandmama whispered to me.

"Oh, yes, please!" I cried.

So, after Grandmama had agreed a price with the whiskery stallholder, the precious poster was very carefully unpegged from where it had been hanging, rolled in paper as soft as a handkerchief, and handed over to me. I was speechless with joy.

17th March 1900

I forgot to mention that before leaving for the train station yesterday Gran took Henry and I on a short sight-seeing tour. She wanted us to take a look at a very strange and unusual new tower. It is known as the Eiffel Tower and juts high into the sky on the south side of the river. I am not quite sure what its purpose is because no one can live in it – it has no walls and is very narrow at the top – but it is quite splendid to behold.

I have clipped my poster to the mirror in my bedroom. It will inspire me.

6th April 1900

Henrietta's invitation arrived this morning to the Earl and Lady Londonderry's ball. It is to be held on

24th May, 1900 at their home, Londonderry House, Park Lane, Mayfair. She ran up and down the stairs with it clasped to her bosom as though she had just received the greatest of news.

"I will meet every titled person and politician in England," she cried with joy. Well, that's better than swooning over Archie Marsh I wanted to say but I was careful not to make any comment which might spoil her good mood.

Grandmama was less thrilled. "Undoubtedly, Lady Londonderry is the queen of British society and it is perfectly right that Henrietta should go. However, although she wishes so dearly to be present at such a gathering, she must not be blinded by all this pomp and circumstance. The Marchioness is extremely powerful. She charms and manipulates almost every gentleman in office as well as those who aspire to be in the government, which is all very well – each of us to our own battle – but it is not that kind of power I wish to see you young girls, or indeed any woman, aspire to." Here, Gran paused and sighed and took hold of my hand, holding it tight and seemed to be considering matters so deeply that she began to frown. "I wish that Thomas, your father, was more … less… He's very conservative, dear."

"Is that bad?" I asked her.

"What? No, no of course not. It's that … if Millicent, your mother, were here… She was less of a conformist… Still, better to see Henrietta out there in society than sitting at home like Sir Vincent Andersen's dull wife who does nothing but eat cakes all day long. We women cannot deaden our sensibilities, Flora. We have much to do in the world, dear and… Oh, I had wished more for Henrietta!"

I wasn't entirely certain what Grandmama was worrying about, but her remark about Papa troubled me. And her mention of my mother surprised me because it is so unusual for her to be mentioned by either Papa or Gran.

22nd April 1900

My birthday. Fifteen today. Nothing special has been planned. Still, Father had said that the trip to Paris was my present given to me early, and it was unforgettable. I would simply adore to be in Paris now.

99

A rather splendid exhibition has just opened. It is everywhere on the streets as well as the exhibition houses such as the Grand Palais. It is known as the *Exposition Universelle* and there are paintings by modern artists from all over the world. There is also a moving pavement – can you imagine such a thing? – a monumental fair and a giant Ferris wheel. Oh, it would be too divine to return there now.

10th May 1900

Horrid guests to dinner this evening. Lord Duncan from the Colonial Office and his wife, Lady Duncan. Grandmama and Henrietta were both out for the evening, so there was only Father and me. I wish now that I had stayed in my room.

Lord Duncan said of Mary Kingsley that she keeps company with black people and, "it is whispered, even allows some of that kind to visit her."

"How could one respect such a creature?" sniped Lady Duncan. "She is a disgrace to the British. She even sets herself against the Colonial Office thinking that she knows better than they how to run West Africa."

"Yes, what my wife says is true. Miss Kingsley actually wants the place to be governed by the traders. Really, she is quite ludicrous."

"It is hardly surprising," Lady Duncan, who seemed to be relishing this gossip, added. "After all, she is the illegitimate child of a serving maid who her father married only days before she was born. Her blood lacks class and breeding, that is obvious. Why else would she entertain the notion that Blacks have anything to say that is worth hearing? Anyone can see that they are of a lower caste and intellect than us."

"She came here for dinner," said Father. "Shortly before she left on her last trip to Africa. I supposed that she must be a supporter of the vote for women, but I had no idea that she keeps company with negroes. If I had known, I probably would not have invited her to eat with us."

When Father said that, I rose from the table and asked to be excused. I have never spoken to a dark person but what Father said made me feel sick. It is true what Grandmama told me, there are horrid things about Britain. Miss Kingsley is a kind and brave person. I hate to hear people speak so ill of her and those she befriends when she is not here to defend herself.

12th May 1900

I related to Grandmama what Lord and Lady Duncan had been discussing at dinner with Father. In return, Gran explained to me that it is true that Mary Kingsley has been battling with the Colonial Office because she does not approve of the way they want to run West Africa. Then she quoted something that Mary had written a few years ago, after one of her trips to Africa. "I feel certain," she had said, "that a black man is no more an undeveloped white man than a woman is an undeveloped man."

"You see how important our battle for the vote is, Flora. A world ruled exclusively by white men who believe themselves to be superior beings is a dangerous one. It is a world built on prejudice and lack of respect."

"But it was not only the men saying those things. Lady Duncan was equally nasty."

"I suppose we should not judge her too harshly. She is not thinking for herself. She is simply mouthing what she has heard voiced by others. A woman like that is not interested in discovering life or finding out for herself what the world has to teach and offer her. Hers is a mindless existence. Of course she and her husband oppose Mary; she is courageous. She is too honest for them and she is not afraid to recognize that everyone, whether they be black or white, male or female, have something to offer the rest of us."

"Even Lady Duncan?"

Grandmama laughed. "Yes, even Lady Duncan. You have learnt a lesson from her narrow-mindedness, have you not?"

I nodded.

"And, no doubt, if she allowed herself to be more open to life, she would discover qualities about herself that might surprise her."

I would love to travel in Africa and make cinematograph pictures there. I want to be open to life and make new discoveries every day!

20th May 1900

The newspapers speak of nothing but victory in the South African Boer War. The British garrison in the town of Mafeking has been saved. It seems that all of England is celebrating. In the East End of London, people are hanging out bunting and banners. Even Father's warehouses are flying flags. Britain is proving yet again to the world just what a powerful nation it is. As I passed the kitchen this morning, I overheard Cook say to Jonesy: "Makes yer proud to be British, don't it?"

22nd May 1900

Last night, Henrietta attended her first society ball. She arrived home in a carriage in the small hours of this morning, she told me later, exhausted but "still spinning with pleasure". Her gown, which was the palest of pinks and was decorated with fresh roses, was a huge success. I think she must have been complimented greatly for she has been rushing about the house as lively as a cricket all afternoon. I must admit that she did look breathtakingly beautiful. Grandmama gave her the most elegant diamond earrings as her coming out gift.

I will agree to come out *only* if my gift is a cinematograph which, of course, I couldn't wear to a ball! But I could take pictures of the ball and of all those who attended it…!

3rd June 1900

Henrietta has been to five balls in almost as many days. She sleeps in till the afternoon because she is so tired and then, after a brief canter through Hyde Park for fresh air and exercise, returns home to prepare for that evening's entertainment. Last night, she danced four times with Archie, she announced at luncheon today. So, he's still hanging around then!

4th June 1900

Our home was worse than a train station today with all the comings and goings and preparations for Henrietta's presentation to Queen Victoria at Buckingham Palace this evening. Grandmama has accompanied her and they spent *hours* discussing how to walk and then curtsey. Henrietta was practising her curtseys to Bassett who howled and barked and ran to hide beneath one of the chairs in the dining room. The sight of him, glowering from between chair legs, and then Henry shouting and getting cross with the poor thing sent Jenny and I into gales of laughter. It all seems extremely silly.

Before Henrietta left for the Palace this evening she came in to my room.

"Wish me luck," she said in a very nervous voice. She was dressed up in a glorious white satin gown and a flowing train that goes with it, clutching a bouquet of flowers. "I'm terrified."

"No need to be," I said. "You look divine." Which she did. "Will you still be able to curtsey with all those clothes on?"

"Don't, Flora, why must you be so horrid!" she cried. "You make me twice as nervous." And with that she was gone. I expect I shall get into trouble for upsetting her which I hadn't meant to do. It's just that I find it hard to take it as seriously as she does. Still, my sister is wondrously beautiful.

5th June 1900

Well, it all went off swimmingly at the Palace. Thank heavens! According to Henry, there were more than 300 young ladies being presented and she was number two hundred and something or other! What an absolute bore it must be for Queen Victoria to sit there while a procession of young ladies files past. Each one pauses in front of her while their names are announced, then curtseys to her twice before moving along. I don't quite see the point. I think I must be what is known as the "black sheep of the family"! I am amazed that all this stuff interests Grandmama. What has it got to do with winning the vote for women? It does not seem like equal rights to me. Do young men go through the same rigmarole? No, they go into the army instead!

This evening at dinner, Henry was describing the interior of the Palace. She claims that the nicest part is the entrance. All the entertaining salons are enormous, she said, and filled with brightly glowing chandeliers. Well, they would need to be spacious to receive so many debutantes.

Still, there is only the Court Ball this coming Friday and then the important dates will all be over. And life will be back to normal. Henry's coming out into society will have been achieved.

6th June 1900

I saw in this morning's copy of *The Times*, which Papa had been reading at breakfast, that a dock strike began yesterday morning. It seems that it has been caused by a contracting firm who have refused to hire labour from outside the dock gates. Angry dockers walked off the jetties shouting about weakening the power of the unions.

I wondered why Father had been so sullen at dinner last night. I have no idea what effect this will have on his company but judging by the frown on his forehead when he set off for work today, I feel sure he must be troubled. Poor Papa, he seems to be having a rather difficult time of it. I do wish that there was some way in which I could help, but he so rarely shares his concerns and I feel unable to offer my love and compassion because I fear he will reject me. Would it be different if my mother was still alive? Would he talk to her?

How different people's worlds are. Henry is flustered at the prospect of the Court Ball, Papa is worrying about who will unload his ships and how he will protect his merchandise and the dockers are angry because they fear their jobs are at risk.

If the newspapers are to be believed, the contracting firm who refused to hire the labour force is working *for Father*. Yesterday, the situation worsened when the contractors locked out the strikers of the day before, who then broke into the docks and called to the men who were still working to put down their tools. They wanted every single docker to stop work and to strike with them. Most of the dockers followed the call, but a few didn't. This caused disagreements. A couple of fights broke out and the police were called again. I asked Father this evening about what was happening and he said that the strikers were troublemakers and they would be punished.

"How?" I asked him.

"We are bringing in workers from elsewhere. The strikers will lose their jobs."

Suddenly, I recalled the image of that bearded docker I saw on the quay all those months ago who was being knocked about by the police. I suppose he must have been a troublemaker too.

8th June 1900

"Well, the band strikes up its opening notes and the ball commences with a dance known as Royal Quadrilles. Queen Victoria led it, of course, but she didn't dance for very long because she is fearfully old and rather dumpy. Still, once she was on the floor, every other member of royalty, including all guests from foreign royal families, were allowed to dance. Lord, it was splendid. All those great dignitaries swirling and turning while the rest of us looked on. Then, only when that dance had been concluded, were we all entitled to take a turn. It was the most enormous fun. Of course, when you take the floor, if any members of royalty are dancing, you must respect a certain distance. I was danced off my feet. Whirling and turning in the arms of so many young men! In fact, I barely remember the names of some of those who requested my hand on the floor..."

While Henrietta was recounting the itinerary of her evening at the Court Ball, I could not help noticing the expression on Father's face. Although he was

111

listening, or trying very hard to affect an air of interest, I felt that his thoughts were elsewhere.

I know that he would do anything in the world for Henry. She is his very special girl, I am aware of that, and he encourages and believes in these society affairs, but he was troubled, I am sure of it. It must be to do with this wretched strike. Now that Grandmama is less occupied with Henry's social calendar, I shall try to talk to her and find out what is going on.

I am glad it's Saturday tomorrow. Father can stay home and rest.

9th June 1900

Saturday or not, Papa went off at the crack of dawn this morning. I don't know where to and he didn't say anything about when he'd be back.

Gran, Henry and I breakfasted together. Then, after breakfast, Henry set off to stay with friends of Gran's outside Oxford who are holding a grand ball at their country estate this evening.

I was glad to have some time alone with

Grandmama. It seems ages since we talked and I needed an opportunity to ask her about Father. We had luncheon together and then went horse riding in Hyde Park.

No wonder Father has been depressed. The union workers stopped work in support of the strikers on Thursday. In retaliation, the contracting company working for Father has started to employ outside labour. Now, the situation is very serious. Grandmama says that under these conditions, the struggle will not get resolved. She thinks that it will most likely spread to all the other docks.

"Your father's company are bringing in strike-breakers from all over England. Some are even being shipped in from Ireland and Holland. They are housing them all on ships and in sheds at the ports, paying them handsomely and feeding them three full meals a day, which is a great deal more than the regular dockers ever received."

"Lord, it must be very hard for Father," I said as we rode beneath the flowering chestnuts in the park. I was feeling terribly concerned.

"Why do you say that, Flora?"

"Because it will be very expensive for him to employ so many labourers who are not part of the strike."

"It is one way of looking at the situation."

"Why? What other way is there?" I asked in surprise.

"One might also consider how those strikers' families are going to survive without money to buy food."

I fell silent. I had not considered such a thing, at all.

When we returned to the house, Father was home, supping a whisky in the drawing room. He seemed to be in a rather good mood, greeting us with the news that Pretoria, in South Africa, has surrendered to British troops. He talked of the celebrations that were taking place down at the docksides. They began at eight this morning, he said, "At our docks. I ordered every vessel of the fleet we had in port to hoist flags from stem to stern and from foremast to mizzen. During the course of the day other ships followed suit so that, by the time I left at five this evening, the entire dockside was covered in bunting and looked like a party event."

"Such outstanding patriotism, Thomas! Well, you have certainly given the strikers something to worry about. Excuse me, I'm going to get out of these riding clothes," declared Gran who then strode from the room.

I followed up the stairs moments after her, confused by this exchange between her and my father. He had been happy by his news of the day, it seemed, and for a reason that I did not understand, his recounting of it had made her cross. Might it be that Gran feels the celebrations are out of place because the strikers' families have no money for food? I am not quite sure.

10th June 1900

Terrible, terrible news. Gran received a telegram this morning to say that Mary Kingsley died of enteric fever in Africa on the third of this month. Grandmama is awfully shocked and very upset. I also feel quietly saddened and I could not help remembering her promise to me of a signed copy of her book which I never received. Such a selfish thought on my part!

20th June 1900

According to the newspapers, there are celebratory processions everywhere through the East End of London. Apparently, they are sponsored by the *Daily Telegraph*. The newspaper has arranged for collecting boxes to be handed out everywhere. Money is being collected for the widows of soldiers who have died in the war in South Africa. These collections seem to have done far better than the boxes which are to help feed and support the strikers' families. Many of the people collecting for the striking dockers have been charged with breach of the peace and taken to court.

In the East End, the pubs and the local inhabitants have given generously to the war and the war widows but not to the strikers or their families. Gran says that the dockers will find it difficult to hold out much longer. These demonstrations and the lack of support for their cause will force them back to work.

22nd June 1900

It's peculiar to be a part of a country at war when the war is so far away. Still, people argue all the time in the press and at the dinner table about it. It seems that there are many who oppose it. For my part, I don't really know what to think. Except that I hate the idea of people killing people and when I remember how horribly those savages were treated at the Great Exhibition, I cannot see that power over anyone is such a good thing.

24th June 1900

A most extraordinary and wonderful thing happened this morning! I received a small parcel which had been stamped in South Africa. I tore open the brown paper wrapping and discovered that it was from

Mary Kingsley; the book she promised me all those months ago. In it she has inscribed in ink:

Dear Flora,
Thank you for your interest in my little book. I hope that it may inspire you to set off along the route of your own travels, your own path and destiny.

May I be so bold as to advise? Well, my advice is: create opportunities for yourself. Make those moving pictures you spoke to me so passionately of. They will be a lasting document of a time which will pass all too soon.

I wish you success and look forward to the next opportunity we have to talk together.
Yours,
Mary Kingsley

My heart beat so fast when I read her words to me. The idea that she had taken my dreams seriously made me flush with pride. She must have posted the packet just before she fell sick. I look forward to reading her book and shall cherish it deeply.

25th June 1900

A month's stay in Suffolk has been arranged for our holidays in August. Father has rented an estate near a small town called Yoxford, which is not too far from the sea. Grandmama is not going to come with us. "Too busy, dear," she says, "to go gallivanting about the countryside in the heat."

For my part, I do not greatly look forward to going because there is not a great deal to do there, aside from reading which I can do here and riding which I can enjoy in Hyde Park. I am not attached to nature, having decided that hunting and shooting are not my favourite pastimes. I prefer the city. Still, we will travel there in Father's automobile so that will be fun. I can't quite see the point of summer holidays. Does that mean that I shall end up obsessed with work like Father? We have hardly seen him in weeks. I suppose we must blame the strike for his continual absence.

26th June 1900

A woman turned up here today. When Jones answered the door, she requested to speak with Father who, he informed her, was not at home. "I won't go, till I speak with 'im," she insisted in a very loud and rather bad-tempered voice.

Miss Baker and I were descending the stairs when we heard this exchange. We had just finished a horrid German verbs class, at which I had fared rather badly, and were on our way to the dining room for lunch. I hung back to find out what was going on and who the rather scruffily dressed woman was.

"I wanna see Bonninton. My 'usband works for 'im at the docks."

"Is Grandmama at home?" I asked of Jones who shook his head.

Miss Baker pulled at my sleeve, saying, "Flora, this is none of your affair."

But I would have none of it and stepped up to the door. "Can I help you?" I enquired of the woman who, when we stood face to face, I realized was a great deal younger than I had originally supposed.

She was a little taken aback and I don't think she fancied discussing her concerns with the likes of me, a person so young and ill-equipped. So, I tried to reassure her by telling her that I was Mr Bonnington's daughter and would be happy to pass on any message she wanted me to give to him.

"You're just a bleedin' kid," she scoffed.

"I am fifteen," I asserted, a little hurt by her dismissal of me after I had thought to be considerate and caring.

"Fifteen, blimey! I got boys your age out working. When they can get the work, that is, and get paid for it. Shows what class does, eh? And an easy life."

"I think you should come and eat your lunch, Flora," chided Miss Baker.

"If you would like me to pass on a message to my father, I will willingly do so," I reiterated.

"Right then, Miss. You can tell your father that we're starving on account of him and his rotten cruelty. You tell him that he's a cold-hearted so and so. Five kids, I've got. I'd like to see your mother put up with what I got on me hands."

I reeled with shock at her words and the sharpness

with which she had spoken them, and I certainly did not tell her that I have no mother.

"Baxter's the name." This was yelled like a hurled stone into my retreating back. I barely heard it at the time. I am not even sure now if I have correctly remembered it.

Suddenly, Jones, with his kindly manner was at my side and he led me away.

"Did you hear what she said about Papa?" I muttered. I don't know if any other words were exchanged after that. The next I knew I was walking into the dining room as Jones guided me to my usual seat.

"What was that about?" I asked weakly to anyone who was paying me attention.

"You shouldn't have gone to hear her but now that you did, you don't want to take notice of a woman like her, Miss."

"Why not, Jonesy?"

"She's abusive. A striker's wife, no doubt, with a foul mouth and foul manners," snapped Cook who was delivering a dish of buttered spuds to the table. Her manner shocked me almost as much as Mrs Baxter's.

I barely touched a bite of my lunch and my lessons were a struggle all afternoon, but I fought hard not to expose the extent to which the exchange at the door had unsettled me. Above all, not because the lady who called herself Mrs Baxter was ugly in the manner in which she spoke – which she was – but because, and God forgive me for thinking let alone writing this, I dreaded, and still do, that there might be a grain of truth in her outburst.

I cannot discuss these feelings about Papa with anyone, not even dearest beloved and wonderful Grandmama. For some inexplicable reason, I feel a real and deep longing to be in the company of Mary Kingsley. She has been in my thoughts ever since I returned upstairs to my room this evening. I have now put her book with its ink-inscribed dedication to me on my pillow at my side. I have been weeping for the loss of her and yet she is a woman I met but the once and I cannot help feeling that my tears are not for her at all. If I could have any wish in the world right now, it would be to have my mother sitting here calmly, in my room, on the edge of my bed, and me kneeling at her feet, with my head in her lap. I long for her in a way I have never known before; I long for her to stroke my hair and listen to my confusions. And to reassure me that my father is not a cold and cruel man.

17th July 1900

The strike is over. Father says that the men are returning to work in "dribs and drabs. They have learnt their place." The whole affair was never more than a "whimper" overshadowed by the great events taking place in South Africa. Father says the failure of the strike is a triumph for the employers. The men will accept the terms and salaries they are offered now with a little more gratitude. "It has taught them their place and they will think twice next time before they challenge the gentlemen who give them work."

I feel less at ease about it, not having forgotten the incident of "the thief" at the port. And that woman, Mrs Baxter, who came to our door.

I have also been reflecting on Grandmama's reaction to Papa when he told his story about ordering all the flags to be hoisted the length and breadth of every ship in dock. Is it possible that his intention was not to celebrate the achievements of the soldiers at war, but to take the attention away from the dockers, to weaken their cause? No, it could not

be. How can I think such thoughts about my
own father?

20th July 1900

We have passed a very jolly few hours. An outing to
a West End theatre this evening where we saw a
performance of *The Man of Destiny*, written by the Irish
playwright, George Bernard Shaw.

During the interval, Grandmama took me by the arm
and led me off, away from Father and Henrietta saying,
"I want to introduce you to someone. Come with me."

Standing at the foot of the stairs which reached up to
the dress circle was a young woman, not much older
than Henrietta, engaged in conversation with two others.

"Christabel, this is my granddaughter, Flora
Bonnington."

We shook hands and the lady, Christabel, said to me
that she hoped to meet me again. "Your grandmother
speaks very proudly of you. Perhaps you will come to
one of our meetings, will you?"

I nodded, feeling rather shy in their presence.

"Deeds not words, Violet," she said to Grandmama as we stepped away.

"Who was that?" I asked as we left the three women to their conversation and made our way back through the throng.

"Her mother is a friend of mine from years back. I met her when she was still a young girl attending her first suffrage meetings. In those days, she was called Emmeline Goulden. Later, she married and became known as Emily Pankhurst. And the lady you have just been introduced to, Christabel, is her daughter."

"What did she mean by her remark to you, 'deeds, not words'?"

"I will explain, but not now. Look, your father and Henrietta are calling us. The play is about to recommence."

I glanced in Father's direction once or twice during the performance. He was smiling and looked as though he was thoroughly enjoying himself but when I asked him later what he thought of the play he said that it was not his cup of tea. "I prefer something a little more patriotic. He's a bit of a troublemaker that Irishman, Shaw," he said.

I suppose Papa was smiling because he is relaxed

now that the strike is over. I wonder what happened to that Baxter family. I would like to talk to that woman again.

24th July 1900

I have been reading Miss Kingsley's book. It is quite wonderful. Her words have transported me to another world entirely. West Africa is a place that in my wildest imaginings I could never have pictured. Think how it would be if I could bring those images alive and show them here in England. Would the likes of Lady Duncan reconsider their cruel comments about the tribes peoples? Could moving pictures bring people closer together, towards a better understanding of the differences between us?

What is inspiring about Miss Kingsley's book is that she went out alone and created her own work. She followed her dreams and turned them into *her destiny*.

Oh, that I might one day have the courage to do such a thing!

3rd August 1900

Grandmother invited me to a meeting attended by herself and many other suffragettes. "You are fifteen. You are old enough to know your own mind and I believe you are ready, but obviously, it is up to you, Flora. Would you like to come along?" I told her that I would like to very much, and so it was agreed.

"As long as your father has no objections, that is."

"Oh, please, don't tell him!" I cried out. The words were spoken before I could think to stop them.

Grandmama frowned. "Why ever not, dear?"

"I would … prefer to tell him later," I stammered. "I would like to surprise him." But my excuse was a lie and I knew it. The truth is, I fear Father will disapprove.

We set off after tea. The meeting was held in a small, rather draughty hall towards the south of London in a place known as the Elephant and Castle. I cannot recall ever having been to that district of our city before. I did not like it much for it was very down at heel. But I have no right to judge it for that reason.

Christabel Pankhurst, the lady Grandmama introduced me to at the theatre a short while ago, seemed to be in charge of things. At least, she was the one who spoke the most and her oratory was given in a very impassioned and rather dramatic way.

"The vote for women is the symbol of freedom and equality," she cried, arms raised above her head. And others called back to her, loudly voicing their agreement. I looked around the place and was surprised to see women with their hair cut short, others who were smoking, still others who had a rather bohemian style of dress, but there were many who looked and behaved in a normal way. Many of the women quite obviously came from the same background as Grandmama and I. One of these was a very kind lady, about Gran's age, who was introduced to me as Millicent Fawcett. I liked her very much. She did not speak a great deal but when she did, her words were carefully considered and intelligent and the others present listened to her with a great deal of respect.

All in all, it was an interesting and colourful mixture of women of all ages, middle-aged like Grandmama, and younger. There were a few men amongst the crowd, too, which quite surprised me because from all that Gran has said to me I had thought that *all* men would violently disapprove of this women's suffrage stuff.

"Any class which is denied the vote is branded an inferior class. Hence women are judged inferior and the inferiority of women is a hideous lie! It teaches men arrogance and injustice!"

"Yes!!" The voices were shouting. Others were cheering and stamping and waving their arms. Their cries rang loudly like bells chiming. The energy was thrilling and I could not help myself being carried along with it. Within no time I was cheering too, although I did not always understand precisely what was being said.

After, hot tea was served from huge pots and we stood around in groups chatting. I say *we* though I did not speak much. In fact, I barely said a word. I was far too fascinated watching what was happening and listening to everyone's ideas and opinions.

The expression, *deeds, not words* was spoken by several of the women. Both in conversation or when they were on the podium addressing the group at large. I thought it must be their motto.

Later, during the ride home in Grandmama's carriage, soothed by the soft clip clop of the horses' hooves against the damply cobbled streets and the gentle sway

130

of the carriage, I asked Grandmama again to tell me what the expression meant. *Deeds, not words.*

"There are many women who feel that the fight has been going on too long. The government is not taking us seriously and now is the time to begin to publicize our cause. Some feel we need to be more unionized to fight for our rights."

"Unionized? What do you mean, Grandmama?"

"That if women banded together in groups and fought together their requests would be listened to. Others, like Christabel, believe we should go out on the streets and begin to march and make ourselves and our grievances known everywhere."

"You mean marching like the dockers have been doing in the East End of London?"

The carriage was approaching Hyde Park. Grandmama glanced out at the wet night and then back at me. "Yes, exactly like that."

"But they lost," I said earnestly.

"Not because they took to the streets. Their defeat was brought about by other circumstances."

"Such as?"

"Support for the Boer War."

"I don't understand," I said, but a part of me feared that I did.

"Most people would rather donate any spare money they have to help our soldiers abroad than help their fellow workers and their families and the less fortunate at home."

"Why?"

"Because the ordinary citizen believes that our British soldiers are fighting to maintain Britain's position as the greatest empire the world has ever known."

"Aren't they?"

"Yes, they are, but…"

"Well, what's wrong with that?"

"Most people do not seem to realize that, in many instances, this country that they feel so public-spirited towards is governed and controlled by those same men who refuse to give them fair wages and better working conditions. It is ruled by the men who keep them poor."

I fell silent thinking on all this. Is that what Mrs Baxter was trying in her own way to tell me about Papa? Is that why Papa requested the flags be flown? If people gave their money to the war widows they would have nothing left to support the dockers and then the men would be forced back to work to support their starving families. The more I thought about it, the more fitting it seemed that women should have the right to vote. It would be one step nearer to a more fair-minded and equal society.

"Well, I'll march, if you will," I replied.

"Done!" laughed Grandmama and hugged me tight.

5th August 1900

Father has cancelled our trip to Suffolk. He says that he has far too much business to attend to here in London and cannot possibly get away.

Grandmother said that he would be disappointing both Henry and I, but we both shouted our disagreements. Henry has been moping for days at the thought of spending a month away from Archie. From my point of view it was one of the few attractions the holiday held for me: no Lydia, no Archie! If Henry ever found this diary and read it, she would hate me for ever more.

6th August 1900

This morning, after Jenny had woken me, while she was pottering around in my room and then preparing my bath, I began to watch her in a way I never have before.

"What are you looking at?" she giggled. I shrugged because I was embarrassed that she had caught me staring.

It was simply that it had never occurred to me before to consider Jenny's position. I don't mean within our household. What I was thinking as I studied her was what would happen to her if things ever got bad for us and Father was obliged to ask his staff to leave. I know that she is only a year or two older than Henrietta – twenty, I think – and that her family are poor and she was born somewhere in the East End of London. She has little, if any, formal education, but I have no idea what sort of wage Father pays her. She can read, I know that too, because I have seen her from time to time with letters which, once read, she slips into her apron pockets like sweets to be consumed later when no one is looking. Are they from a boyfriend? Is she to be married? If Father were to throw her out on the street, which I know he wouldn't, what rights would she have? What prospects? I fear, none.

If I understand correctly, from what one or two of the women were saying at the meeting the other evening domestic servants are not members of any unions. Hence, Jenny has no rights whatsoever.

"Do you have a boyfriend, Jenny?" I asked eventually. She was bending over at the time sorting through petticoats in a drawer.

"Your question is a bit personal, don't you think?" But her response was said with warmth and a glint in her eye. "Yeah, I have."

Then I wanted to ask her how she pictures her future and what, if any, ambitions she has. But I was unsure whether or not she would think those questions too impertinent. Would she judge me horribly inquisitive?

How shocking it is that I have always taken it for granted that there should be maidservants in our house to care for me and my needs, but that their concerns should be of no matter to me.

"Will you leave here and marry your boyfriend?"

She howled with laughter. "He hasn't asked me yet!"

"Do you love him?"

"What do you want to know all this for?"

"I was thinking about your rights, Jenny. You know, if you should ever leave here…"

"My rights!" she scoffed. "Don't be so daft. What rights do I have?"

"That's exactly what I mean," said I, leaping off the bed to my feet. "If you joined the suffragettes…"

"You've gone loopy, you have. Suffra-what?"

"Votes for women, Jenny. Unions for domestic servants. The right not to be kicked out of your job. Fair wages."

"I think you should get in your bath. Your towels are warmed." And, with that, she disappeared from the room, shaking her head and muttering: "rights for domestics, I don't know."

But I had meant it. I shall talk to Gran and see if we cannot persuade Cook and Anna and even Jonesy to accompany us to a meeting.

9th August 1900

Henry has received an invitation, along with Archie and the rest of the Marsh family to go to Ireland to stay at Wyngard, the famous country estate which belongs to Earl and Lady Londonderry. Father thinks that it is a splendid idea and has said that she can go at once. Jenny will accompany her. Our house is a-bustle with activity. Cases and clothes are everywhere as they both prepare for Henry's departure.

15th August 1900

I have been thinking about what Grandmama said in the carriage the other evening, about how we could best publicize the suffragette movement, aside from marching on the streets, that is. And I have had a most wonderful idea! How would it be to cinematograph one of the meetings? Then we could find church halls, institutions, local meeting houses, any place where the windows could be darkened, to exhibit our moving pictures. Women all over the country would be able to find out what is happening. They could hear what the suffragettes are saying and what they – no, WE – are fighting for. Surely, that is more efficient than giving out leaflets or marching? The problem is that I don't have a cinematograph camera. And the cinematograph does not have any sound, so we could not reproduce the discussions at the meetings.

Still, there must be a way to put such an apparatus to this good use, and what a well-found opportunity it would be for me to learn the craft I am so hankering to be involved with!

17th August 1900

Before dinner this evening, alone in the drawing room with Grandmama, I confided to her my plan about the cinematograph. When I had finished, she sat very silently, frowning. Her silence was so long and so considered that I feared I must have said something terribly wrong, until she nodded. Slowly, at first, brow furrowed deep in thought, she eventually replied. "It's a brilliant suggestion, Flora. The question is how can we effectively put it into practice?"

"The first thing is the cinematograph," I replied excitedly.

"No, no, the first consideration is … how on earth do we go about finding someone who could operate the camera?"

My heart sank like a stone in a lake. "Me, Grandmama. I will work it out. That's the whole point!"

She turned to me in astonishment and looked me full in the face. "You, Flora?"

"But, of course!" I cried. How could she doubt me or my idea? My heart was pounding. "You can't take the idea away from me Grandmama, you can't! It's what I have been dreaming of all year!" I was all but yelling at her because I was so intensely afraid that my opportunity was about to slip right out of my fingers, stolen by my closest ally.

"Sssh, sssh, dear. I had no idea you felt quite *this* passionately about it."

"But, yes! Yes! I don't want to come out into society and spend hours being fitted for dresses. I don't want to marry a chinless man like Archie Marsh who has more moustache than brains. I want to be a suffragette. I want to be like Miss Kingsley and travel. I want to be like you and care about people and causes! I want to do something with my life!"

"Hush, child, hush."

I sighed and sank back in my chair. "Sorry," I muttered tearfully, "I didn't mean to shout at you."

"No, your passion is splendid. The question is how to put all that energy to practical and positive use. Even if we could find a cinematograph camera for sale..."

"I could return to Paris and ask that lady director working for Mr Gaumont..."

"Alice Guy?"

"Yes, I could ask her to teach me."

"Flora, you are fifteen years old. This is not an apparatus that you learn to use overnight. The suggestion is excellent but your ideas for the execution of it are impractical."

I wanted to weep and sorely wished that I had never mentioned it, even to Gran. I should run away. Go to Paris and sit outside Mr Gaumont's studio until they agree to take me in and teach me the art of cinematographs.

I *will* go to Paris!

20th August 1900

"Well, Flora, I have been making enquiries and, it seems, we might be able to find one of your cameras right here in London." This was Grandmama talking. She had asked Jonesy to fetch me to her study. When I entered I found her at her desk, her *pince nez* dangling from a long golden chain. She was waving a sheet of paper at me which was covered with lines of illegible handwriting. She spoke in a matter-of-fact manner. It was as though she were describing the most direct route from point A to point B on one of the underground train lines, while I, amazed, was barely able to take on the reality of what she was saying.

"I think we should contact this gentleman. Wait, I have his name here somewhere. Where is it? Ah, yes, here we are! This is the fellow, Mr Birt Acres. He has been exhibiting his pictures at the Royal Photographic Society. They have given me his details so I think we should telephone him and ask to meet with him, don't you?"

"Oh, yes, please!" I cried.

21st August 1900

Grandmama spoke to Mr Acres on the telephone early this morning. He has advised her that there is a colleague of his, a Mr RW Paul, who is making and selling cinematograph cameras here in England. It is he who has been producing them for the French illusionist George Méliès.

Now, all I have to do is to try and persuade Father to buy me one!

Mr Acres has invited us to the Royal Photographic Society to see his film. I am thrilled. So is Grandmama.

"Well, Flora, I am looking forward to this outing. I hope that I shall be as taken with these moving pictures as you are."

Oh, I so want Gran to be inspired, and then she will want to support me and plead with Father on my behalf.

23rd August 1900

Thank heavens we did not go to Suffolk. If we had, Gran and I would have been denied the pleasures of today's outing. This afternoon, we visited Mr Acres at the Royal Photographic Society. And what an event it turned out to be.

Mr Acres has cinematographed a series of photographic images which he has entitled: *Rough Sea at Dover*. As with the earlier pictures I saw with Miss Baker, each frame follows on from the last in fast succession to create the idea of movement. The subject today was waves crashing against a sea wall and, my word, the illusion was magnificent. The waves crashed and the spray exploded in the air into white clouds of foam. It was so realistic that we actually feared we might get wet! Grandmama was as taken with the whole business as I am.

"I almost believed I was standing alongside that sea wall," she whispered to me as our host switched off his projecting machine.

Our afternoon was made even more special because

we had the viewing to ourselves; with Mr Acres, of course.

Afterwards, we took tea together. Gran was bursting to know all about it.

"Well, I congratulate you, Mr Acres. Those pictures in motion are most lifelike. Please, will you be so kind as to explain to us exactly how the whole business operates because I would like to purchase one of your cinematographs."

"You will need a projecting system to accompany it, Lady Campbell."

"Yes, yes, of course. Whatever is needed. And an operator, of course."

"No," I hissed, but no one paid me any attention. When Gran is enthused by one of her good works or projects she pays no heed to anyone and, this afternoon, that included me.

"There are one or two methods in operation at the moment. We are working with the one that is known as '35 millimetres'."

"Why such a name, Mr Acres?"

"Because, Lady Campbell, that is the width of the film we are using. Please, let me show you."

Mr Acres led us from where we had viewed his work through to a small area which he called the projection cupboard. There, with the apparatus in front of us, he expounded on several technical matters. I have to confess that, try as I did to follow, I was soon lost. He demonstrated how the movement of the film is made possible. The film, which rather resembles a long length of ribbon, has holes punched into each of its two borders. These clip in to sprockets which are attached to a kind of wheel. The wheel turns and with it go the sprockets which carry the film along. In this way the film is moved forward. It is quite ingenious!

Gran seemed to grasp the specifics of it all without too much difficulty. She was certainly asking a great many questions, such as who had created the idea of film in lengths of ribbons. An American named Kodak, was Acres's response. She enquired after the price of the film, then the cost of this and that and wrote down various figures and names, even an address or two.

On our way home in the carriage, Gran was still scribbling notes. "There is a great deal to learn, eh, Flora?" I only nodded because I knew that my idea of owning a camera and simply taking pictures had been proved to be rather naive, but I was thrilled that she was so taken with it all.

26th August 1900

Six days ago, one of Father's steamers, *India*, bound home from Java laden with 85 tonnes of sugar went down in heavy seas off the east coast of Africa. All passengers and crew seem to have escaped by the lifeboats so, thank the Lord, no casualties have been reported, but Father's entire shipment has been lost to the oceans. He must have known about it for a day or two because it was reported in *The Times* but he has said nothing to us which makes me fear that the loss is a big blow to him and his company.

I cannot possibly mention the cinematograph now! How selfish of me to think only of myself.

30th August 1900

Henry and Jenny are returned from Ireland. Clearly, they have had a splendid time. Henry is filled with the beauties of the Irish countryside and she never stops dropping the names of this or that Duke or Lord who she lunched with or took tea with. All that aside from several princes she was invited to dance with.

"So, did you find yourself a handsome beau? Will you marry a prince and become a princess?" I asked her, jokingly.

But to that she replied in exaggerated surprise, "Why, Archie Marsh is my beau. Who else do you suppose, you silly girl? You understand nothing of true love, Flora Bonnington!"

How I hate it when she patronizes me!

Jenny tells me that she has "never seen the like in sumptuousness as the Londonderrys' country estate. I could have slept in the stables; the place was that posh and comfy."

14th September 1900

Archie and Henry are to be married! Yes! Father has approved the match. What a positively dreadful business! I feel sure that if Henry waited, she would find someone far more entertaining to spend the rest of her life with. Oh, well, it's her life. I overheard Grandmama in the library expressing similar doubts to Father. I think his response to her upset me more than the thought of the marriage.

"Violet, Archie is a titled gentleman of means and an excellent catch. I feel that, under the circumstances and for Henrietta's sake, we should not allow this opportunity to slip by."

Lord, it makes marriage sound as tedious as cricket! I shall have none of it!

20th September 1900

Grandmama was talking to me of converting a part of her Gloucestershire estate into a studio for the use of the art of cinematography! I am so excited that she is enthused.

"It will be an expensive proposition, Flora, but I do believe there is something in your idea of using it to teach people and to show them marvels taking place elsewhere in the world. The pictures we saw the other day were very exciting, but you are quite right, Flora. One could go further. I am going to have a word with your father about it."

29th September 1900

Father is absolutely furious with me. Before Grandmama went out this evening, she recounted our plans to him. I had been intending to accompany her to a suffrage meeting but he forbade it and summoned me to his study. I seem only to be invited there when I am in trouble.

"What on earth do you think you are playing at?" he asked me brusquely.

"I don't know what you mean," I replied.

"This talk about moving pictures."

"But it is what I want to do," I answered nervously.

My response must have infuriated him because he slapped his hand hard against his desk and began to shout at me. "This is idle nonsense, Flora. I will have no daughter of mine involved with any of it, do you hear me?"

"But, Papa, there is no harm in it." Arguing was a fatal mistake. I had intended to simply state my case but it only enraged him further.

"How dare you speak back to me!" he shouted. He seemed unreasonably upset. "You are a young lady of breeding. I had thought that it was some fanciful notion that would pass. Do you think that I would ever allow my daughter to move in such a world? The idea that you harbour thoughts of wanting to work at all is bad enough, but in among vulgar folk who have been born to vaudeville and theatre and the like. It is a working class amusement, Flora. Fairground entertainment, nothing more. Do you think I want you to end up with circus people and freak shows. It is disgusting! I should never have allowed all this talk of women's rights in this house. I should have put my foot down and insisted that you behave yourself and concentrate your energies, like your sister, on the things that matter. I am ashamed of you. You will be thought of as little better than an actress and you will bring disgrace upon our family name!"

"But Grandmama is…"

"Go to your room!" he shouted.

I was stunned by the force of his temper. As I turned to go, he told me that I am forbidden to leave the house without his approval and consent. I have spent the evening alone by my fireside, crying.

1st October 1900

I could not sleep at all last night and, eventually, got up and went downstairs to the kitchen for a glass of milk. As I was passing by the library, I heard voices from within, speaking sharply. I had not intended to eavesdrop, but the door was ajar and my attention was caught by the conversation taking place. It was between Father and Grandmama.

What I heard has shocked me so deeply. I wish I had not been witness to it because now I am at sixes and sevens and I have no one to confide in. I need to try and remember the exchange word for word, as best as I can, to make some sense out of it and to calm the torrent of feelings that have arisen within me and distressed me since the hearing of it.

Father was the one talking as I was passing, before I stopped to listen. He sounded irritable and his words were spoken in an impatient way. He said something like, "Violet, if you have no further use for your estate, then why not offer it to Henrietta and Archie as a wedding gift?"

Grandmama was calmer. "No, Thomas, I will not. Your treatment towards Flora is quite unreasonable and if you so stubbornly and cruelly refuse to encourage her attempts to expand her young mind and to seek out her creative direction, then I intend to assist her myself. Besides, I am in agreement with her. I believe these pictures in motion have a future and, if intelligently developed, could do much good in the world. Like Flora, I also want to share in this new discovery. You should be proud of your daughter, Thomas, not punishing her. She has a fine imagination and it should be encouraged."

"In the same disastrous way you encouraged Millicent. Is that what you are trying to tell me?"

Even from beyond the library door, I could almost hear the shock in Grandmama's silence.

"If it hadn't been for you, Violet, egging your daughter on to works that were quite inappropriate for a young mother and a pregnant woman, I believe that Millicent would still be alive today."

I could hardly believe what I was hearing. My heart was pounding and my head was swimming in a sickly way. I was shivering with cold.

"How can you even contemplate such a thought, let alone voice it?" Gran spoke slowly, in a considered manner, but I could tell from her deep gravelly tone that she was hurt or angry and was fighting to remain calm. I longed to open the door and rush in and speak out for her, but I could not bring myself to move; I was shocked rigid.

"You know yourself that what I am saying is true. Millicent wore herself out supporting you and your preposterous, no, dangerous, suffrage schemes. Her place should have been here at home at my side, caring for me and her small daughter, Henrietta. Instead of which, you filled her head with nonsense, rushed her from one meeting to another where useless females filled their empty heads with ideas about votes for women and blathered foolishly about opportunities to study the law or medicine. The very notion of a woman as a doctor goes against the natural order of things. I find it obscene. Such ambitions should have no place in a woman's world…"

"Thomas, you are…"

"And now, you are doing the same with Flora.

Flora's tragedy is that she resembles her mother too closely. I had hoped that she would change as she grew older. I kept silent, thinking it would pass, but that was wrong of me. She has inherited her mother's passion. And you encourage her. But, this time, I refuse to stand by and watch while her head is turned by you and your compatriots; women who do not know their place or are simply sad unmarried creatures who have nothing better to do with their lives!"

"I cannot believe what I am hearing, Thomas. I have always judged you a reasonable man..."

"The moment my shipment of gold bars arrives from Africa and I have received payment for the delivery and sale, I shall refund to you every penny you have invested in my company, and you will be free to leave this house. Now, if you will excuse me, I have work to do."

There was a long silence – I supposed Gran was taking on the reality of all that Father had just told her – followed by her response, softly spoken. I detected no anger in her tone but, I fancied, a certain sadness.

"Unlike others less fortunate, I am not in need of the money, Thomas. If you want to return it, you may do so, whenever you see fit, and I shall accept it as your wish to settle all outstanding financial matters between us, but, please, do not jeopardize the stability of your business for my sake, particularly in the light of your recent losses at sea. In the meantime, I shall make plans to leave this address, but I shall do so discreetly and in my own time. I shall try to choose a moment which will not encourage gossip nor cause unnecessary distress to the household. Goodnight."

I heard Gran's footsteps crossing the study and I fled – not to the kitchen where I had been headed, but back upstairs to my room – before the door opened and I was discovered.

Now what? A life without Gran is too ghastly to contemplate. Am I really so like my mother? How I wish I could talk to her, just for fifteen minutes! And what of my father? I have never heard him utter such cruel and unkind thoughts before. Never. I want to write that I hate him, but I cannot. I do not.

18th October 1900

Our house, our home is cheerless. Nothing has been mentioned by anyone about the exchange I overheard all those days, weeks ago and I cannot bring myself to let Gran know that I am party to it all. Actually, the days are a curious mix of moods; joylessness on the one hand and happiness on the other. Henry scoots about chirping merrily, making plans for her spring wedding, blind to the family undercurrents. Meanwhile, dear, wonderful Gran goes about her affairs in a quiet gracious way, but her eyes have lost their sparkle. I can see it. And what of Father? He has grown even more distant and unapproachable.

I want to burst with the weight of it all. Might this state of affairs pass? I pray that it will. I hope that Father and Gran can find a way to heal the rift between them and that we remain none the wiser, (officially, that is). Still, the idea that Father could blame my grandmother for the death of my mother is horrible.

28th October 1900

Yet again, London is proving itself the capital city of the "world's greatest empire". Everyone is talking about the Boer War because a ship named the *Aurania*, carrying soldiers returning from a tour of duty in South Africa docked in Southampton yesterday. These soldiers, who sailed from Cape Town on October 7th, have been involved in combat and are to be given a hero's home-coming. The soldiers left London for Africa last January – I wonder if any of them was nursed by Miss Kingsley?

A parade through the streets of London is being arranged by the Lord Mayor of London. The soldiers known as the City Imperial Volunteers have been brought by train to Paddington Station instead of more directly to Waterloo because Paddington is the Queen's station. It is more prestigious and the surrounding neighbourhoods are less seedy and down-at-heel.

It is to be called the City Imperial Volunteers March and Father says we must go because it is history in the making. Archie and his sister Lydia will be accompanying us. Of course, we will not line the streets and wait with the crowds for the passing of the procession. Apparently, there is to be a reception which will be held at the Guild Hall. I believe the Queen will be in attendance, and Father has been invited. He is planning to take us in his automobile. We will follow the procession and, after, we will attend the reception. I have no idea if Grandmama has been invited but, in any case, she is not coming with us.

"Why not?" I asked her when I found her alone in the study answering her mail.

"Because I have something else to do, dear."

"Couldn't I come with you?" I asked her. "I'm sure I'd rather."

"No. Your father is perfectly right. It is history in the making and, one day, you will be grateful that he took you along," she replied without enthusiasm.

"Pictures in motion and suffragettes are also history in the making and you know it. I don't care about the war any more than you do."

"You are wrong, Flora, I do care about the war. I care that people are dying needlessly. And I rejoice for each of those soldiers who has returned home safely, as well as for their families. And I believe that if women were given the vote there would be less fighting, less need for bloodshed."

"Are you really going to leave us, Grandmama?" I asked, almost without realizing what I was saying. She looked up from her writing, pen in hand, and stared at me with an expression which was both surprised and suspicious.

"What makes you ask such a question?"

"I overheard you and Papa arguing in the library."

Grandmama placed her pen slowly, thoughtfully, on to her desk. "Were you eavesdropping?"

"No! Of course not. I couldn't sleep. I was on my way to fetch a glass of milk."

"Sit down, Flora," she said, pointing to a chair which I drew up alongside her, next to the writing bureau. "Your father is right to care for your future welfare, and I … I was wrong to fill your head with ideas that you are too young to be a party to…"

"That's rubbish, and you know it!" I was on my feet, flustered and tearful. I felt as if I was losing my only ally and that, in a way, Gran was betraying both me and her principles.

"Don't lose your temper, Flora. If you want to discuss this, then you must behave like a young lady and not a petulant child."

Her manner was sharp and chiding and made me want to cry, but I took a deep breath and sat down again.

"I am fifteen and a half. Henry is barely more than three years older than I am and she is getting married. So, if she is old enough to know her own mind…"

"In my opinion, she isn't!"

"I want to know what happened to my mother. And why Father holds you responsible."

"That is for him to tell you, Flora."

"But you know he won't! I have a right to know."

"Very well," she sighed. "Your mother caught pneumonia in the last days of her pregnancy. Her body was not strong enough to fight the infection. She grew weak and died shortly after you were born. There, you have it."

I sat staring at her, waiting for her to expand on what she had said but she did not. "Now, please, Flora, I must continue with my letters."

"Why did she catch pneumonia?" My grandmother made no response. "Please, Gran. Was it something to do with you and the suffrage movement?"

"Yes."

"What happened?"

Again, Gran sighed. She did not want to be pushed into a corner but she was too gracious to reject me and I had to know.

"She was canvassing with me. She shouldn't have

been. She was eight months pregnant with you, but that was why she felt so strongly about the cause, don't you see? Women did not have sole custody rights over their own children. She believed passionately that, in the case of the death of a husband, every woman has the right to bring up her own children in the manner that she sees fit. Thomas forbade her to continue with our work. He said it would tire her. She did not heed him. We were walking from house to house, knocking at people's doors, trying to explain to them what it was we were fighting to achieve, and to ask them to sign our petition. The weather grew dark, the sky louring and an unexpected downpour drenched us both. Even with my carriage waiting at the end of street, we got soaked to the skin.

"By the time we returned here, Millie was shivering and chilled through. Cook and I put her straight to bed. Thomas was not at home. I sent immediately for Doctor Hubbard, but there was nothing he could do for her. Within a matter of days, she had developed pneumonia. She must have picked up the virus somewhere while we were out canvassing. You were born, a little prematurely but not seriously so, and five days later Millie, weak and feverish, died. So, in a way, your father is right. I was to blame and I have no right to encourage you along the same path."

"No, Gran, you're not to blame. You didn't force my mother, did you?"

Gran shook her head and smiled.

"And you are not forcing me. You said yourself that it was something my mother believed in passionately. How would Papa have felt if, after the loss of my mother, someone had come to him and said: *You do not have the legal right to bring up these children without a guardian who we consider* is *better able to look after them than you are?* Don't you think he would have lost his temper and fought for his rights, too? I think what my mother did was courageous and I am only sorry that I cannot tell her so. And as for forcing your ideas upon me, it was me who introduced you to moving pictures, so there!"

Grandmother leant forward and stroked my face. "You are so like her," she whispered, and I swear there were tears in her eyes.

"It would be terribly wrong of me, and a betrayal of the memory of my mother, not to follow the path I passionately long to follow. But what you have told me has also helped me understand Papa a little better. He has always been so distant with me. It has hurt me so much. I feared he did not love me the way he loves Henrietta. I have always feared that he thought less of me and that I disappoint him in a way I could not understand, that I have let him down."

"No, Flora. I think that when he looks at you, he sees the beautiful woman he loved so deeply and, though he has never for one second blamed you, he lost her when you came along."

I nodded, kissed Gran on the cheek, whispered a barely audible *thank you* and left her to her letter writing.

29th October 1900

Today is the City Imperial Volunteers March. I have promised myself that I will be agreeable and do whatever Papa asks of me. I shall even be as nice as pie to Lydia and Archie.

30th October 1900

Yesterday was LONG! We set off from home a little after ten with Papa in his automobile. Archie sat next to him in the front and I was seated in the middle between Henry and Lydia. Every square inch of London seemed to be taken up with people. I had not imagined how crowded it would be. At every turn there were soldiers in their various uniforms lining the routes. Military bands were performing *Soldiers of the Queen* as well as other patriotic airs. The public were everywhere, herded together along the pavements, packing the taverns and coffeehouses. It was almost impossible to creep forward at any pace at all. Working people, delighted by the prospect of an unforeseen day's holiday, were perched in the branches of trees while dozens of children straddled the shoulders of their fathers, pointing in our direction. The routes were a living, moving sea of faces and bodies, cheering and eating and waving. It was very impressive, in a way.

Passing along Fleet Street, we caught sight of many

journalists eager to find themselves a story. The down-at-heel pubs in that vicinity and the cafés were packed and noisy and doing a roaring trade. I longed to stop and take a tour and hear what they were all so busy talking and laughing about. Few seemed to have their eyes on the passing procession of City Imperial Soldiers who, whenever I caught a glimpse of one up ahead, looked quite bemused by the furore. I was transfixed by the number of people who had turned out for this event. Everyone was shouting "God Save our Queen" or "Rule Britannia" or "Long Live the Great British Empire", waving flags and bits of cloth or throwing their hats in the air, any old thing.

Suddenly, in the midst of all this, Henry said: "I suppose those soldiers are being rewarded for massacring hundreds of darkies." And then she went on to tell us, as though the two thoughts were directly connected, that she had read an advertisement in *Queen, the Lady's newspaper*, offering the services of a group of nigger minstrels called The Happy Darkies. "They can be hired for private parties," she said.

"Oh, how nasty to have darkies wandering about loose at a party! I would be so fearful," cried stupid Lydia.

"Of course, they are not real savages, Lydia,"

explained Henrietta, in an exaggeratedly patient way. "They are ordinary decent white men with their faces blacked up. I believe it is all the rage now. I think it would be a simply splendid and novel idea to have them perform at our wedding. Archie agrees and we intend to try and persuade Father to employ them for us. What fun!" I turned my attention elsewhere, remembering the promise I had made to myself – to be agreeable and nice to everyone. I concentrated hard on the world passing before my eyes beyond the automobile. There are times when I wonder if Henry and I were really born into the same family. The idea of such an entertainment struck me as horrid but my mind was distracted from such thoughts by an accident somewhere in front of us as we approached Ludgate Circus. I could not see what had happened but there were ambulance men everywhere and the whole procession seemed to have ground to a halt. I think it was because we were barely moving that I spotted the banners and was able to read the lettering so clearly though, try as I might, I could not see who was carrying them. But there they were, waving in the wind high above the sea of heads, clear as daylight. I was on the point of shouting out, but contained myself for I knew my joy would not be well received. There, in amongst the throng of people, were the placards with slogans saying VOTES FOR WOMEN and others with IF WOMEN HAD THE VOTE, WE WOULD VOTE AGAINST WAR. I thought of Christabel Pankhurst and her words to Grandmama, *Deeds, not words, Violet*, and wondered if she were there somewhere in among the crowds bearing her message for all, including our Queen, to see. I felt warm and proud inside. I tried to kneel up and peered hard into the people but they must have been more than a hundred deep. It was impossible to identify anyone in particular. Might Gran be out there somewhere? I asked myself.

A little further along, amidst much pandemonium, I spotted one or two other placards. Their messages seemed to be protesting against the city council: The LONDON COUNTY COUNCIL WANTS CHANGES AT THE EXPENSE OF THE RATE-PAYERS, one stated. And another: LCC SHOULD CARE FOR THE HEALTH AND LIVING STANDARDS OF *ALL* ITS INHABITANTS. Archie interrupted his discussions with Papa and turned back towards us, saying, "Look, see there, Henrietta. The Socialists are making trouble again. Even on a day filled with national pride such as today, they cannot keep from complaining."

I bit back my desire to say something and thought instead of how wonderful it would have been to capture this day, the throngs of the people, the protests, this famous city of London in full sail, on my dreamed of cinematograph. It would truly be history in the making. So many different points of view. I tried not to dwell too long on these thoughts for the fact that I will never have my camera only makes me heartsick and frustrated.

Still, what a fine tale to tell and, although the moving pictures would be in black and white, I should entitle it: *Our Colourful Empire*.

Finally, after St Paul's Cathedral where the Lord Mayor and some city sheriffs in brilliant red coats awaited the procession, we made our way to the Guild Hall. Upon arrival at the Guild Hall yet another band struck up the first notes of *God Save the Queen* and dozens of soldiers dressed in khaki began to troop inside, ready to be honoured. And so we followed on.

By the time the reception was over, I felt as if we had been to war ourselves! When we returned home, completely exhausted, Gran was not there. I thought nothing of it at the time. Only later, at dinner, when I asked after her and Father remarked that she had been called to her estate in Gloucestershire, did I begin to feel afraid.

After supper, I sneaked along to her room to take a look at what was there. Many of her possessions had been removed and her wardrobe was half-empty. My heart was beating so fast as I ran downstairs in search of Jonesy. Father and Archie and Henrietta were in the drawing room so I knew I could have a quiet word with him. Jones was in the kitchen polishing Father's shoes. If there was news, he would be bound to have heard it.

"Where's Gran?" I asked him.

I could tell by the strained look on his face that he knew.

"Tell me, Jonesy, please. Is she visiting her estate, or has she left us?" Without a word, he stuffed his hand into his trouser pocket and pulled out an envelope which bore my Christian name. Recognizing the writing, I ripped it open at once. Jonesy stayed at my side.

My dearest child,
You caught me at this letter yesterday when you found me in the drawing room and I suppose I should have been less cowardly and just downed pen and told you the truth, which is that I am leaving Cadogan Square for a little while. Do not

be alarmed or upset for I feel sure that matters will resolve themselves quickly, and we shall all be reunited again before too long. Please do not blame your father. This is my choice and not of his commanding. I have work to do for the movement which, I fear, would only embarrass him. I also feel in need of a short holiday, though, heaven knows if I shall find the time to take one.

Work very hard with your studies, for a good education will stand you in good stead, whatever path you choose, remember that. Be brave and patient — your time will come — and I promise to buy you a cinematograph for your seventeenth birthday.

Gran xx

I looked up at Jones who must have known the contents for his expression was as bleak as I felt broken-hearted. My seventeenth birthday! Lord, that is eighteen months away.

"Do you know where she has gone?"

He shook his head.

5th November 1900

Today, tonight, is Guy Fawkes Night. On this night, everywhere in England, folk light bonfires and burn a guy. A guy is a stuffed thing, like a big floppy rag doll. It is an effigy of the man, Guy Fawkes, who in the year 1605 tried to blow up the Houses of Parliament, home to the British Government, in a plot which failed and led to his execution, The Gunpowder Plot. It is not an event that we, as a family, have ever celebrated. So, why do I mention it in my diary now? Because I feel that Father and everything he stands for should be blown up. Britain, the Empire, the lack of rights for women, keeping me away from what I care for and love, driving Gran out of our home. No, I don't want to blow up my father. I love my father. It is what he believes in that I want to destroy. Surely I am not alone? Whether I be born into an aristocratic family or I come from a very poor one, surely other young girls of my age experience the frustrations I am experiencing? If I had been sent away to school rather than educated by a governess at home, even though I really, really like Miss Baker, I would have other girls of my age to talk to. But would I dare voice the thoughts I am thinking?

Before dinner this evening, I was so downhearted by everything that I pleaded with Jenny to help me cut off my hair. She stared at me, as she sometimes does when she thinks I am talking like a wicked fairy who eats frogs. "What are you asking?"

"It is the latest fashion," I protested. "I want my hair cut short. Just below my ears, I think." And so, Jenny, reluctantly, with a little assistance from me, chopped off my locks.

My appearance is most unladylike and, I think, rather splendid, but what a to-do this evening when I went down to dinner. You might think by the expression on everyone's faces that I had sliced off my head.

"What have you done to yourself?" asked Papa with a face as white as a sheet.

"I have cut my hair," I replied, in my most matter of fact manner.

"Oh, Flora!" shrieked – literally shrieked – Henrietta. "No, I don't believe it! How could you have done such a thing! You will be a disgrace at my wedding. Worse, you will bring disgrace upon our family. How could you have been so thoughtless and selfish!"

"Henry," I answered in a tone which I hoped might calm her. "Your wedding is not until March. If I wish it, my hair will have grown again by then. Please don't be so upset. It is my appearance, not yours."

"You are a witch," she screamed, and ran from the dining room.

"I will see you in my study after dinner," pronounced Father, as he does when he has something monumental to say but prefers to save it for later so as not to disturb whatever is currently in progress, which, in this instance, was his dinner. We ate in silence, until Henry returned and made such a theatrical display, addressing all her conversation to Papa just as though I did not exist at all.

Jones, when he came in to serve at table and caught sight of me, nearly dropped the platter of lamb. His face, trying not to express his shock, made me want to burst out laughing, even though I knew I was in for big trouble later. In fact, my encounter with Father was nothing out of the ordinary. He asked me what I had been thinking of and why would I want to deliberately spoil what he described as my "pretty feminine looks".

My only response was to shrug. I was unable to say the things I was bursting to say. Father is a very imposing figure and when he is angry, he can be quite daunting. I suppose I had hoped that I would be able to pour my heart out to him. Part of me was longing to confide in him but, as it was, I just stood there with my head bent, silent and unhappy. My punishment is the same as before. I am housebound and can only go out with his permission.

"And that, young lady, will only be given when I am satisfied about where you are going and with whom. Now, go to your room and stay there."

10th November 1900

Father has dismissed Jenny. I cannot believe it. On account of my hair. I found her sobbing her heart out in the upstairs laundry room.

"But, how can he possibly blame you? I never mentioned to him that you had anything to do with it," I assured her.

"When he asked me outright, I was obliged to tell the truth and admit that I did the chopping of it. Then he said to me that, as your maid, I should have been keeping an eye on you, not encouraging such carryings on. He told me to be out of here by Friday. He'll give me a month's pay."

"That's ridiculous!" I cried. "Please, don't be upset, Jenny. I'll make him change his mind. Do you have a place to stay while we sort it out?"

She shook her head and wept more bitterly.

I ran along the corridor in search of Henrietta, but she was not in her room. Suddenly, it struck me how apart we had grown. When had we last confided in one another or giggled like sisters? It was my fault. I was to blame. She must have sensed how much I dislike Archie. She must have been hurt by my aloofness, by my unwillingness to share in her happiness. While I was thinking all of this, I was running to and fro, opening doors, peering in rooms, trying to decide what I could possibly do. There is no way in the world we can allow Papa to dismiss Jenny. She is part of the family and, more importantly, she HAS NO RIGHTS. How could I have been so selfish as to involve her in my prank, my rebellious act against my father? If Gran were here none of this would have happened. I thundered down the stairs in search of Cook or Jones, threw open the kitchen door and there they both were, looking grim. The news had obviously reached them. Jenny had probably told them first, and their sympathies would lie with her. Whatever loyalty they felt towards me or my family, or any other individual within it, they were the employees and we were their employers.

I could see by the expression on both their faces as they glared at me that already something had changed. They had taken a step away, a step towards the safety of their own ground, and I was not welcome to intrude upon it.

"Where's Gran?" I asked. But I could tell at a glance that they were neither of them willing to get involved. Leaking such information to me – the troublemaker, the rebel – could cost them their jobs.

"She's the only one who can plead for Jenny," I pressed. "I telephoned Gloucestershire but she's not there."

Still they did not respond. I stared in shock for an instant and then fled the room. Miss Baker. Where was Miss Baker? I glanced at our grandfather clock in the hall. It was almost ten. Any second now she would be arriving. Normally, she would have been here by this time. She was late. Or had Father sacked her as well? I hovered in the hallway and, as she opened the front door, I all but pounced on her.

"Flora!" she shrieked. "You gave me a scare."

"Where's Gran?"

She looked completely bemused. Her blue eyes were dancing and staring in a very puzzled way. "What's wrong?"

"Papa has dismissed Jenny. I need to find Gran."

"Jenny? But why?"

"Because of me and my constant talk of the cinematograph and because I cut my stupid hair and I hate Archie Marsh and I DON'T KNOW WHERE GRAN IS!!" I was yelling and sobbing, out of control.

Miss Baker took me by the hand and led me through to the drawing room. She took off her coat, folded it neatly and placed it on the arm of the sofa. "If it were about the cinematograph and the moving pictures, I think that he would have asked me to leave, don't you? I don't know where your grandmother is. But have you spoken with anyone at the Suffrage Society?"

The words were like magic to me. "It never even occurred to me to ask there. But, of course. I'm going there at once." I rose to leave but before I had taken a step Miss Baker took me by the arms.

"Flora, wait! You know that you are forbidden to leave the house without permission. Do you wish to have the entire household thrown out on the street? Stop, take a deep breath and let us think this through in an intelligent manner."

"I have to get a message to her. She must come back and beg Father to change his mind. If he wants someone to pack their bags and leave, then I will."

"Be quiet, Flora. Stop this nonsense and let me think!"

Reluctantly, I sank back in to a chair.

"I have it," she said. "At midday, I have a mathematics lesson with Henrietta. Until then, I am supposed to tutor you. History, followed by geography. I will set you the work I had prepared for us to study today and then I will slip off. If, for some completely unexpected reason, your father should return, then you must tell him – it's a lie, I know it – that I was forced to go to the dentist. But, you must promise me to stay here and study. If you disobey me, you will make things impossible for all of us. And, Flora, I do not approve of lies on any account, but I cannot bear to think of Jenny without employment, do you understand me?"

I nodded, and then shook my head. "I am coming with you," I said.

"No!"

"Yes. I have caused this situation and I want to do my best to sort it out, and I want to see Gran."

"Flora—"

"Telephone Papa, *please*, and request permission for us to leave the house."

"Flora, you are putting my job in jeopardy, as well."

"No more than if you had gone to the dentist. Telephone him and I will call for a carriage."

Father agreed that Miss Baker could take me on a trip to the Natural History Museum, and so we escaped.

The Society headquarters were situated in a small mews house in Chelsea. Grandmother was not there but Christabel Pankhurst was. I requested to see her and, at first, was refused but when I explained my dilemma, the young lady at reception agreed to call her. Christabel recognized me at once and then, to my utter amazement, embraced Miss Baker as though they were old friends.

"Deeds, not words," they muttered to one another as though exchanging their secret code.

Christabel sat with us in the reception while I explained our plight. Once our story had been told, she agreed to get in touch with Grandmama immediately who, she informed me, "is holidaying in Venice, Italy. Meanwhile, the society will organize a bed for your housemaid, Jenny, until matters are resolved", which, she assured us, would be very soon.

December 1900

Matters have been resolved and in a most admirable fashion. Gran returned from Venice and has moved back in with us at Cadogan Square, denying that she had ever intended to leave for any length of time. She received a warm and hearty homecoming from us all. Her intention had been to speak with Father on Jenny's behalf, but, I am pleased to say, I had already resolved the situation. After Miss Baker and I returned from the London Headquarters of the Suffrage Society, I went looking for Jenny and found her slumped like a bundle in a corner of the laundry room. Her face was puffy and blotched red from crying and I felt guilty and ashamed, having come to understand the real delicacy of her situation and the trouble I had caused.

"You have nothing to fear, Jenny," I told her, intending to comfort her. "You will be taken care of."

But my words did nothing to alleviate her distress. She wept on, telling me that she could not return to her parents, her boyfriend had not proposed to her and in any case matters were not going too swimmingly between them and she did not believe that he wanted to marry her and she wished now that she had never met him in the first place. "I'm jobless and homeless," she wailed.

I was responsible and I knew that it was for me, not Gran, to put the affair in order, and I resolved there and then to do so. When Father came home, distracted and filled with work concerns as usual, I requested the time to talk with him. At first he was grumpy, as though I was interrupting his train of thought, but when he saw my face and the gravity of my intent, he nodded and led me through to his study. I sat down, facing him. My heart was beating like a kettle drum. Papa must have sensed my fear and discomfort but he did not make it easy for me.

"I'm waiting," was all he said.

I knew this was my moment and that if I did not open up to him now and stop fighting him, the opportunity might get lost and we might never be friends or understand one another. There was so much to say I hardly knew where to begin, but I took a deep breath and started, falteringly, to pour my heart out to him. He never once interrupted, so I had no notion of how my words were being received, but on I went. I recounted how I had overheard the dispute between him and Gran and how I had blamed him for her departure. I tried to explain to him how deeply I wanted to pursue a career of my own and not be married off like Henry. I apologized for cutting my hair which had been an act to spite him and I made it clear that Jenny had been in no way responsible. Still he said nothing but his face, I was sure of it, had softened a little and he was listening earnestly and patiently.

Finally, I came to my mother. Father's hands which had been resting clenched on his desk were withdrawn and I knew that I was treading on delicate ground. I begged him not to hold me responsible for her death, nor Gran either. And I begged him not to judge me harshly because, apparently, I resemble her.

"Please, don't judge me in an unkind way because I don't aspire to the things you believe in. I am head-strong, Papa, I know it," I said, "and perhaps that is not always such a good thing. On the other hand, I believe passionately in what I want to achieve and without such passion and drive nothing in the world can be changed. Please, Father, don't deny me my chance."

"And what is it exactly that you want, Flora?"

"I desperately want to make moving pictures and,

like Gran and mother, I want to fight for a redefinition of the roles available to women in our society. And I want almost most of all, for us – you and me, Papa – to be friends." A lump caught in my throat, and I fought back my tears. "I want us to love one another."

He said nothing. We sat either side of his desk in silence, like strangers, but he never took his eyes off me. Two islands floating in different directions, until he whispered so softly that I barely heard him, "Come here."

I got up, shakily, and moved round the desk to his outstretched hand. He took hold of me, pulled me towards him and hugged me so tight that I thought I would stop breathing. "Thank you," he murmured in my ear.

The upshot of the whole affair is that Jenny will not be leaving us. In fact, after Christmas, she will be accompanying Miss Baker and I to Paris where I am to be educated for the coming year. Obviously, we will all be returning for the spring holidays and Henry's wedding to Viscount Archie Marsh.

In the meantime, Father has written a letter to Mr Léon Gaumont and to his lady director, Alice Guy, requesting part-time lessons for me in the art of cinematography. We are awaiting their response.

Historical Note

The Early Victorian ideal of womanhood placed women very firmly in the home, looking after their husbands and children. But by 1899, 62 years into Queen Victoria's reign, changes were taking place. It was now not uncommon for middle-class women to be employed as teachers, secretaries or civil servants, or even as doctors in a few cases. Oxford and Cambridge Universities had women's colleges, and although those universities did not allow women to be awarded degrees, London University granted full membership to women in 1880. Married women could legally own property after 1882 – prior to this everything belonged to their husbands. Some women had been granted the right to vote in local elections by a Local Government Act of 1869, and many took part in local politics. In contrast to how we live today, these might sound very small advances. But there is no doubt that women were enjoying new freedoms at the time Flora would have written her diary, gained in part by the various campaigners for women's rights. However, women still did not have the right to vote in parliamentary elections.

The campaign for women's suffrage began in the 1860s. A small group of wealthy women, who met regularly at Langham Place in London, published the *English Women's Journal*, which included articles on extending the right to vote to women. The London Society for Women's Suffrage was formed, and soon afterwards similar groups were founded in other parts of the country, which were brought together in 1867 as the National Society for Women's Suffrage.

John Stuart Mill included women's suffrage in his campaign when he became an MP in 1865, and his famous book, *The Subjection of Women*, was published in 1869. In it, he wrote:

I think that almost every one ... would admit the injustice of excluding half the human race from the greater number of lucrative occupations... Under whatever conditions, and within whatever limits, men are admitted to the suffrage, there is not a shadow of justification for not admitting women under the same... Women require the suffrage, as their guarantee of just and equal consideration.

It's important to remember the "conditions" and "limits" John Stuart Mill mentions: very few people could vote in the early nineteenth century. Two Reform Acts, in 1867 and 1884, changed some restrictions on who could vote so that many – though not all – working-class men were granted suffrage. As Flora records in her diary, the differences in rights afforded to male and female was not the only inequality at the turn of the nineteenth century.

The few working-class women who were involved in the campaign for suffrage would have found themselves still without a vote if the same financial and property restrictions that applied to men were also applied to them. Many suffragists felt that the demand for a vote for women should extend to demanding votes for everyone, irrespective of class and financial status, while others disagreed. This and other arguments caused different suffrage groups to form, split and disagree with one another. The Women's Franchise League, founded by Elizabeth Wolstenholme Elmy in 1889, was one of the first suffrage groups which actively encouraged working-class women to join, and working-class involvement in the suffrage movement did increase after about 1890.

In 1897, Millicent Fawcett led a joint meeting of suffrage societies which agreed to form the National Union of Women's Suffrage Societies (NUWSS). The NUWSS, the largest of the suffrage societies, continued campaigning by lobbying MPs, holding meetings and publishing journals and pamphlets, and went on to organize a series of marches. The first of these was known as the Mud March. It was held in February 1907 from Hyde Park to Exeter Hall. Although this march, with its banners and numerous brass bands, was a non-violent event it marked the beginning of militant action by the suffragettes. It was the real start of "Deeds not words".

Timeline

1832 Reform Act means that the right to vote is extended to include the more prosperous males only.

1833 Slavery is abolished in Britain and its Empire.

1837 Victoria becomes queen, aged 18.

1840 Queen Victoria marries her first cousin, Prince Albert of Saxe-Coburg-Gotha.

1854 The Crimean War begins, and continues until 1856.

1866 John Stuart Mill presents a women's suffrage petition to Parliament.

1867 London Society for Women's Suffrage is formed. Reform Act grants the vote to more British men, though many working-class men are still excluded. All women remain excluded.

1869 Municipal Corporations (Franchise) Act allows single women property owners the right to vote in local elections. *The Subjection of Women* by John Stuart Mill is published.

1870 Richard Pankhurst, the husband of Emmeline, drafts the first women's suffrage bill. More suffrage bills follow throughout the 1870s.

1872 Central Committee for Women's Suffrage formed.

1876 Alexander Graham Bell patents the telephone.

1877 Queen Victoria is made Empress of India.

1882 Married Women's Property Act allows women to keep their own property after marriage (until now, a married woman's possessions were legally owned by her husband).

1882 First Boer War (in South Africa) begins.

1884 Reform Act increases the number of men entitled to vote. The women's suffragists' proposals for the Act are defeated.

1889 Women's Franchise League is founded by Elizabeth Wolstenholme Elmy.

1893 The manufacture of motor vehicles begins in the UK.

1894 Parish Councils Act extends the vote in local elections to propertied married women, as well as the single women who have been local electors since 1869.

1896 The Lumières hold the first public demonstration in Britain of their Cinematographie, showing their film entitled *Arrival of a Train*.

1897 National Union of Women's Suffrage Societies is formed.

1899 Second Boer War begins.

1900 The Labour Representation Committee (later to become the Labour Party) is formed.
1901 Edward VII becomes King.
1903 Women's Social and Political Union is founded in Manchester by Emmeline and Christabel Pankhurst.

Fashionable evening wear for young women in 1899.

Poster advertising the Lumière brothers' Cinematograph.

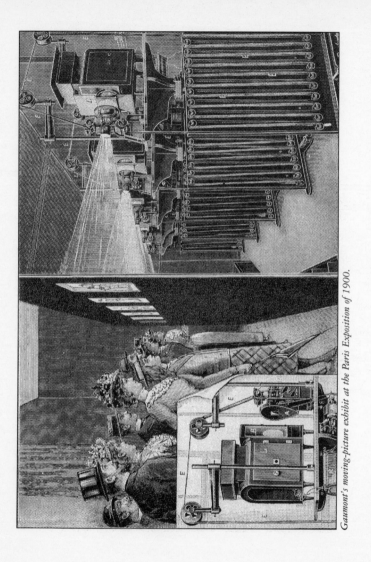

Gaumont's moving-picture exhibit at the Paris Exposition of 1900.

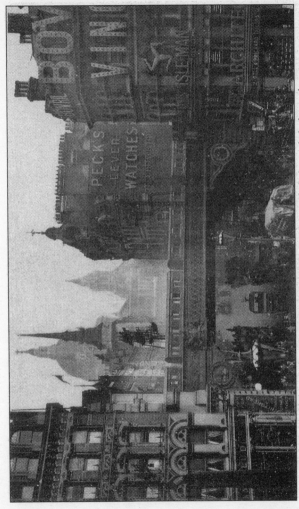

A busy street scene at London's Ludgate Circus in around 1900. St Paul's Cathedral is in the background.

A crowd queuing to see a travelling bioscope show in Cambridgeshire in around 1906.

A gelatine silver print of Millicent Fawcett taken between 1890-1895.

A women's suffrage society office at the beginning of the twentieth century. One of the posters shows a working woman and her children and reads "Breadwinner, Tax Payer, Why Not Voter?".

Unloading a cargo at a London dockyard in 1900.

Debutantes leaving the Presence Chamber at Buckingham Palace after being presented to Queen Victoria. The debutantes all wear long-trained dresses and veils and carry bouquets of flowers.

Traffic in Kensington, London, in 1903. Cars were first manufactured in the UK in 1893 and were becoming increasingly popular during the early years of the twentieth century.

Picture acknowledgments

P 192   Young ladies' evening wear, *La Mode Illustrée*, Mary Evans Picture Library

P 193   Cinematograph poster, *Magic*, Mary Evans Picture Library

P 194   Gaumont's exhibit at the Paris Exposition, *La Nature*, Mary Evans Picture Library

P 195   Ludgate Circus, Mary Evans Picture Library

P 196   Crowd queuing in front of a travelling bioscope show, Mary Evans Picture Library/Barry Norman Collection

P 197   Millicent Fawcett, Mary Evans Picture Library/The Women's Library

P 198   Oldham Women's Suffrage Society office, Mary Evans Picture Library/Fawcett Library

P 199   London Docks, *Living London*, Mary Evans Picture Library

P 200   Debutantes at court, Everard Hopkins in the *Illustrated London News*, Mary Evans Picture Library

P 201   London traffic, FS Spence in the *Illustrated London News*, Mary Evans Picture Library

My Story.

the hunger

The Diary of
Phyllis McCormack, Ireland 1845-1847

10th November, 1845

Horrible! Horrible! The rot has destroyed most of
the potatoes which were wholesome and sound when
we dug them out of the ground. Da opened up the
pit this morning and found it filled with nothing
but diseased mush. All we have left to eat are those
that hadn't yet gone underground.

"Six months provisions are a mass of stinking
rottenness. Where has it come from?" Da kept repeating
all morning. "Disease will take us all," he drawled.

My Story.

VOYAGE ON THE GREAT TITANIC

The Diary of Margaret Anne Brady, 1912

Monday 15th April, 1912

It was after midnight, and I could still hear people moving about in the passageway. Before I had time to go out and join them, there was a sharp knock on my door.

I opened it to see Robert. His eyes looked urgent.

"Good evening, Miss Brady," he said. "You need to put on something warm, and report to the Boat Deck with your life belt."

Miss Brady? When I heard that, I felt alarmed for the first time. "A routine drill," he said. "No need to fret."

I knew he needed to get on with his duties, so I found a smile for him and nodded...

"You'll not want to take your time, Margaret," he said in a very quiet voice.

It did not seem possible, but maybe this was not a drill.

My Story.

The Crystal Palace

The Diary of
Lily Hicks, London 1850-1851

17th April, 1850

The Crystal Palace is more wonderful every time we go,
with coloured light everywhere, so airy and delicate, but
strong. Not like a house, solid and heavy and shadowy,
solid to the ground. Like being inside a diamond it is,
or a fairy palace. Master has made a miracle,
everybody says so. And as for the exhibits inside, there
are more and more every day, 10,000 they say. We saw
French and Belgian lace and English embroidery today,
so fine the Queen can't have better – shawls and baby
gowns and waistcoats, and Irish double damask
tablecloths with shimmering ferns and flowers woven in.
I was near crying with pure delight it was all so lovely.

My Story.

BLITZ

The Diary of
Edie Benson, London 1940-1941

Friday 30th August, 1940

Last night was very still and clear. As Dad went
out for the evening shift, he looked up and said grimly,
"If they're ever going to come, it'll be on a night like this."
And sure enough, the first air-raid warning came at a
few minutes past nine. Mum was out at the ARP post,
and Shirl, Tom and I were huddled together in the
shelter with Chamberlain.

Shirl's teeth were chattering already. "Cor blimey!"
she said. "What's it going to be like in the middle
of winter? I've got no feeling in my toes at all."

I could see Tom was about to open his mouth and say
something clever when we heard the first explosion,
and then two more following close on the first one...

My Story.

My
Tudor Queen
The Diary of
Eva De Puebla, London 1501-1513

4th November, 1501

I hardly like to make a mark on the beautiful,
blank pages of this book, but I must. Mama gave it
to me as a parting present so that I could write about
this journey from Spain to England. "Don't waste it,"
she said. "Just write the important things." I'm sure
Mama would be impressed by the great procession in
which we have slowly made our way from the West
Country to London. Horses and carriages, litters and
baggage-waggons and attendants, soldiers, courtiers,
ladies, pages, jesters – and Catherine herself,
Catherine of Aragon on her way to wed Prince Arthur,
eldest son of the king of England.